She was in no mood to meet a stranger

Soaking wet and furious, Margo, fully dressed, had just emerged from an unexpected dip in the Villa Romana pool. She stormed off toward the house, her nurse's uniform clinging to her body.

The stranger approaching was tall and very tanned.

"We're not buying anything today," Margot snapped. "And this is private. property."

"Just a minute!" he shouted after her, so that she whirled around to meet a pair of steely blue eyes. "I'd advise you to get out of those wet things."

Margot stared at his red checked shirt, old slacks. "Are you a doctor?" she asked unbelievingly, seeing a black bag sitting near his car.

"No, I'm a parachutist," he mocked, while Margot's temper rose even higher. "And I believe we're going to be working together—unfortunately."

Harlequin Premiere Editions

Harlequin Premiere Editions

AT THE VILLA ROMANA

Anne Vinton

Harlequin Books

TORONTO • LONDON • LOS ANGELES • AMSTERDAM
SYDNEY • HAMBURG • PARIS • STOCKHOLM • ATHENS • TOKYO

Original hardcover edition published in 1977
by Mills & Boon Limited

ISBN 0-373-82109-3

This Harlequin Premiere Editions volume
published October 1981

Printed in U.S.A.

AT THE
VILLA ROMANA

CHAPTER ONE

MARGOT WALSH awoke as the finger of bright sunlight fell across her eyes. She had told Giovanna, the maid, never to draw the sunblind over her window. Most Italian houses were like mausoleums from eight in the morning until sundown in summer, but Margot still did not fear the sun even after four weeks in Italy. She shook her dark, straight hair, slipped into a robe and tiptoed from her room and across the hall to George's room.

She was a trained nurse and he was her patient, the reason for her being here in the Villa Romana on the rugged Tuscan coast of Italy. George's room was darkened and he was sleeping; he had called her at one in the morning, and after she had attended to him he had been so wakeful that she had persuaded him to take a mild sleeping pill. Now he slept deeply and the rest of the household was still. Nobody dreamed of going to bed before midnight at least, or getting up until eleven or so, apart from Mr Whitham, who left the house at seven forty-five. Only Giovanna would be astir in the kitchen and her husband, Salvatore, in the grounds. Both, who were full of song by nature, had been trained to keep silent until the family they served eventually yawned themselves into soporific activity.

Margot crept back to her room and slipped into a swimming-costume. She was fairly tall with a slim, attractive figure with eyes the grey of doves' wings.

Salvatore had once told her as she sat reading in her white nurse's uniform, 'The Signorina is like a swan.'

'Yes,' she had thought, 'but graceful and calm as it looks, the swan has to paddle vigorously to even exist. Nobody ever sees how hard it really works underneath.'

She let herself out of the house and ran to the marble swimming-pool, deserted at this hour. Rows of statues, gods and demi-gods, paraded on either side, and she always touched the figure of Cupid on her way to the shower. Why she touched it so religiously, she didn't know. Because he was the reputed god of love? But love had turned sour on her, which was another reason why she was here at the Villa Romana. Because he was sightless and stricken? But he was really only cold marble and she could not even feel for the little finger which had been broken off during the years of his tryst overlooking the pool. Maybe she touched him for luck, or just out of habit, but it was one of those things she now did automatically, like washing her hair.

She stood under the shower and gasped, always amazed at the coldness of the mountain water which was piped to the villa, and then she dived into the pool, which was heated, and swam her usual four lengths before showering once more and donning her towelling robe. Salvatore appeared dragging a besom, and showing a mouthful of bad teeth. Margot spoke only a little Italian, and Salvatore used a rich Tuscan dialect in any case, but he had a little English he liked to practise.

'Is good day, eh, *signorina*? Sun is shining. Have much work.'

'Me too, Salvatore,' Margot said with a smile, and went off between banks of tree salvias and poinsettias towards the house. The building was old but had been lovingly maintained and had absorbed all modern convenience without losing any of its dignity. It stood in four lush acres of sub-tropical vegetation and was draped in purple and red bougainvillea. A high wall surrounded the villa and one could forget there was a world outside; Margot had been glad to when she had first arrived in the middle of May. Here she was, a nurse with a patient, who had been picked up by an aircraft and deposited, heart dulled with aching, in Rome, again picked up by an imposing dark blue Cadillac and conveyed here to the Villa Romana, where behind its walls she could try to forget Mike—who had said he loved her when he only desired her, and who had laughed disbelievingly when she had said she would like to be married.

'Grow up, girl,' he had taunted her. 'Things ain't what they used to be, you know. I like you a lot and we have a great deal of fun together, but marriage? You have to be joking. What need is there for that?'

What need, indeed? she had thought flatly. Didn't people want to get married any more? Was it something that had gone out of fashion like the bustle? Supposing one wanted children? Was that ridiculous, too, to expect them to grow up with both a father and a mother? She hadn't mentioned marriage again, because she hadn't really known Mike all that long; just long enough to fall in love with him and believe he was in love with her, too. When her mother had fallen ill Mike had been very sweet, taking her home when he was free, and understanding her natural anxiety so that they were more like friends than sweethearts. Then the end had come very suddenly; Mrs Walsh's death had been a great shock to her only daughter. Matron at Merchant Hospital, where both Margot and Mike were employed, had granted her extended leave while she saw to things.

Mike had said things like, 'Don't brood. It won't bring her back.' But how could one help but brood when all within a month one had lost the dearest parent and most understanding friend a girl ever had?

Perhaps they had been closer in that Margot's father had died when she was only three, and that Barbara Walsh had never clung to her only child when she was ready to flee the nest. She had encouraged Margot to become a nurse, even though it meant she would have to leave home, and she had been proud every time Margot passed an exam and went higher up the nursing ladder until she was State registered. She had listened quietly to her daughter, after she had met Mike, confiding that she thought she was in love.

'Being in love is wonderful, darling. Just make sure that you love him as well.'

'But isn't it the same, Mother?' asked Margot.

'Not quite.' Barbara Walsh smiled. 'You can be in—and out of—love a dozen times. But usually you love only once, and that's it.'

'Oh, but I do love him, Mother! I do! I do!'

'I'm sure you do, darling. It'll all work out. Have patience.'

After the funeral Margot didn't see Mike at all. She had to wait until the cottage was sold, and it was not a seller's market. More than half the sum it brought at auction went to pay off the mortgage, and then she was left without a roof over her head and just over four

thousand pounds in the bank. She had to keep on working, and she wrote a very telling letter to Mike, discus-
sing her feelings of depression and insecurity and her
longing for the comfort of his presence. She was to quit
the cottage in a week, and maybe he would come over
for the weekend. People—the neighbours—might talk,
but nothing would happen and they needn't fret. Mike
would understand that she needed simply to be loved;
the thing her mother had spoken of that went beyond
sex.

On the way to the post she had met old Sister Underwood, who was retired but sometimes relieved when
anyone was on holiday or ill.

'I was so sorry to hear of your trouble, Nurse. But you
must get back to work. You're looking peaky—a pity
you missed the engagement party. It would have cheered
you up, and it's not disloyal to the dead to go on living,
you know.'

'Yes, I know I have to go on and get back to work,'
agreed Margot. 'Who got engaged, then?'

'The consultant's daughter, Rose Myers, and that nice-
looking Doctor Verne. I try to be fair, but I do think he
knows which side his bread's buttered, that young man.
He'll step into Sir Leslie's shoes, I shouldn't wonder.
The wedding's supposed to be in June.'

Margot had heard in her head a smashing as of broken
glass, which was her world breaking into fragments.
Some central cell in her brain told her clearly and kindly
that at least she hadn't posted the letter. Her pride could
still be saved. Pitiful pride that comes such a poor second
to love!

'Are you all right, Nurse?' Sister Underwood inquired. 'You've gone quite pale.'

'Oh, yes, I'm all right. I'm just tired. There's been so much to do—and I still have to go to the shops, if you'll excuse me?'

She had walked for an hour, just pacing the streets of the small town which was a kind of dormitory for the big city where Mercha t Hospital was situated; and then, because she knew how hospital grapevines worked, nourishing rumours into facts, she rang up a nurse of her year who also worked at Merchant Hospital.

'Hello, Doris. This is Margot.'

'Oh, hello, old thing! This is my day off and I haven't anything to do. There isn't a decent film on anywhere I haven't already seen.'

'Then why don't you come over here for a meal? I'll make a curry. I won't have the house much longer or be able to entertain at home. You can tell me all that's been happening.'

And so she had had the fact confirmed that Mike Verne was engaged to Rose Myers, who worked as a radiographer at the hospital and was the daughter of Sir Leslie Myers, who was a consultant surgeon and Mike's boss. Of course the two girls spoke of many things, and then Doris asked suddenly, 'Wasn't Mike Verne keen on you once, Margot? Among many others, of course.'

'Of course,' Margot forced a smile, 'and as you say, among many others.' She hadn't known of any others, but Doris was extremely shrewd and must know what she was talking about. She was plain and efficient, one of those observers who are said to see most of the game. 'I haven't seen him for quite some time now,' she added.

'No great loss,' said the down-to-earth Doris. 'I've always thought him a bit of a bighead, myself. He's good-looking, I'll admit, but too ambitious to be human. When are you coming back?'

'I may not,' Margot said quietly. 'Oh, I love the old place, but I've been forced to make the break and now I may look elsewhere. What's to keep me here now?'

'Where will you go?'

'I don't know. But a trained nurse need never be out of work. I'm just thinking things over at the moment.'

She was dashed by the news of Mike's inconstancy, or, to be more honest, her own gullibility. If there had been many girls in his life then he was not inconstant, simply in character, and she had been the one who had stepped out of character and thrown him temporarily, by mentioning marriage. Yet love and marriage were still synonymous to her, who didn't love lightly and meant the words when she spoke them, whereas she realised now that he had been playing the field, and Rose Myers had turned out to be the favourite he was backing in the marriage stakes. With her famous father, and the nepotism that still existed in medicine, Mike had probably made the best bet, if his future as a surgeon was pre-eminent in his plans.

Margot saw the job advertised in *The Times* as she was packing up odds and ends of family treasures to put into storage. A firm of auctioneers was removing the furniture next day.

'Trained nurse required to care for paraplegic boy by English family planning long holiday in Italy. Interviews arranged.' Then followed the name and telephone number of a recognised nursing agency.

Margot read it twice and decided it would give her a breathing space, should she get the job. She rang the agency and was told to go for interview to the London Hilton on Monday next. She had scarcely put the phone down when men came to disconnect it, which made it all look like the hand of fate, somehow. Later in the day she had another visitor, and it was Mike.

She never knew, afterwards, how she was able to look at him. He appeared decidedly uneasy, but she smiled and asked him in.

'Will you have a cup of coffee, Mike, or something stronger? The gas is still on and there's half a bottle of whisky in the sideboard.'

'You've sold the house, then?' he asked.

'Yes. It was difficult, but it's done now. What did you say you'd have?'

'Oh, coffee will be fine. Especially after that awful stewed dishwash we get at the hospital.' He watched her light the gas in the kitchen and put some milk on to heat. She scooped coffee into a percolator and soon it was bubbling. 'Best Blue Mountain,' she smiled. 'I hope it's better than the hospital stuff.'

'Sure to be.' He began to fidget as she invited him to sit at the kitchen table, where it was cosy with the range burning warmly behind them. 'I say, Margot, I hope you didn't think I let you down in your time of need? I was busy—and things happened.'

'Yes. Congratuations,' and she found she could still smile.

'Oh, so you heard?' He looked almost relieved. 'It was all rather sudden, but I've known Rose on and off a long time.'

'I hope you'll both be very happy,' Margot said.

'Well, thanks, old thing! It's just that Rose and I are the same sort of people. We don't look for roses round the door and the patter of tiny feet, at least not for years. She's going to carry on working and——'

He gulped at his coffee which was hot and made him choke.

'I don't know why,' he said, as though to himself, 'I suddenly thought of you as I took you away from your mother's grave, refusing to let go and cry, and then I realised it had been simply weeks and I hadn't been near or heard anything.'

'You were busy getting engaged,' Margot reminded him.

'Yes, and—dammit—I thought you might mind.'

'Why should *I* mind?' Margot asked, almost brightly. 'After all, I wasn't the only girl you'd taken out, was I? You have my blessing. O.K?'

'You really mean that?'

'I mean that.'

'Then I'm happy and relieved. It was good while it lasted, wasn't it, Margot?'

'Now stop thinking about the past or fishing for compliments from your old girl-friends,' she urged. 'Be good to Rose and make her happy.'

Mike reached over and kissed her and the kiss was brotherly. She wished he hadn't done it, because a brother's kiss, after passion's, was water after wine.

When he had gone she found she could cry, not only for him but everything, and long after the tears finished her slight frame was racked with her grief. Then she pulled herself together and continued to do what must be done, somewhat mechanically, determining never to fall in love again if love was such a deceiver. How could one ever be sure of anyone again if Mike, during those emotion-filled moments they had shared together, had merely been whispering feverish, accommodating lies for his own selfish gratification?

On Monday she took the London train and was shown to a large suite on the twelfth floor of the hotel to meet the Whitham family, who appeared overwhelmingly sure of their position as prospective employers.

'She's a bit young, isn't she?' Mrs Whitham asked her husband, as though Margot wasn't there. 'Too young, do you think?'

'Nobody's too young who's got the qualifications, Emmy,' said John Whitham, who was sitting in the apartment helping his wife interview applicants for the job.

'It says here you're twenty-four,' Mrs Whitham went on, looking at a slip of paper in her hand. 'That seems awfully young to me.'

'Yes, I'm twenty-four,' Margot found herself saying, 'and that means I've been nursing for six years. At my last hospital I was due for the next vacancy as Sister.'

'A Sister?'

Margot explained patiently. 'We rise from being nurse to staff nurse and then Sister is the next step. Sister runs the ward, her staff nurse is her first lieutenant.'

'I think the others we've had have been too old, Emmy,' Mr Whitham contributed. 'After all, George isn't going to want some old battle-axe looking after him, is he? Someone nearer his age might be a good idea.'

Mrs Whitham seemed unconvinced. 'Do we like this one, or don't we?' she asked.

There was a little explosion behind Margot's eyes and she spoke before Mr Whitham could answer.

'Perhaps the question is whether or not *I* like *you*,' she said. 'After all, I'm not exactly desperate for a job.'

Mrs Whitham's blue eyes shot wide open and her husband laughed loudly.

'Golly, but *I* like her. You got my vote, dear.'

Margot looked back at his wife, however, where she sensed a certain amount of hostility towards her lay. Whatever the woman's hair had been by nature, it was tinted, now, a bright red. As John Whitham continued to laugh Margot thought she saw through that blue-eyed hostility a look of deep hurt. She spoke directly to Mrs Whitham now, in a quieter tone.

'Isn't it of prime importance what your son thinks of his nurse?' she asked. 'After all, he *is* the patient, isn't he?'

As if on cue the door opened and Margot looked into the eyes of the young man who was to be her patient. He was in a wheelchair, and a hospital porter who had been exercising the lad in the nearby park excused himself and left. A girl and a younger boy slipped into the apartment, but Margot did not take her eyes from the figure in the chair. It was as though he was used to people being embarrassed by his condition and amused himself by staring them out of countenance, but Margot never wavered.

'This is George,' Mrs Whitham said, almost defensively. 'George, come and meet Nurse Walsh.'

'Hello, Nurse Walsh.' George flashed a ventriloquist's

doll smile at her and then wheeled himself further into the apartment. 'I thought you'd have finished with all the interviews by now or I wouldn't have come back. What happened to that fat old frog with the moustache you rather fancied for me this morning?'

'She probably found your charm utterly resistible,' Margot flashed. For the second time she had startled not only herself but everybody else. It must have been her bereavement and then Mike's defection which had triggered this unknown defence mechanism within her into action. 'Will that be all?' she asked Mrs Whitham politely.

'I'd rather like you to take the job,' the elder woman said almost pleadingly. 'I apologise for George, but you see, he hasn't accepted his condition yet. But there he is, and there he's going to stay and he has to be professionally cared for. What do you say, Nurse?'

'I'll take the job,' Margot said, with a slow smile breaking on her lips.

On this warm late June morning Margot dressed in her white uniform and cap, with her navy blue nurse's belt and silver buckle, and ensuring that George still slept she went into the kitchen to breakfast. Giovanna indicated that it was not quite ready, so Margot went out through the kitchen door and climbed the staircase which led to the roof.

From here there was a view of the sea, dancing and sequined in the morning sunlight, and there were four or five boats of the local fishermen on station. She supposed they were fishing for the giant prawns which sometimes appeared on the table at the Villa Romana, but occasionally she entertained a romantic notion that perhaps they sometimes pulled up buried treasure in their shrimping nets and trawls. Maybe a Roman galley had sunk out there thousands of years ago, and even after all this time the sea occasionally gave up valuable relics. Because this Mare Nostrum was a magic sea, and the bays on this Tuscan coast a truly enchanted part of it. It changed its face hourly, depending on the light and wind conditions. On a calm, sunny morning like this it was pearly grey, tinged with pink; by noon it would be a deep, calm blue and in the evening the sun setting behind landward hills would turn it to violet streaked with blood red like an exotic shot silk. It also had its 'Atlantic' days, however, when the west wind drove through the Straits of Gibraltar and stirred everything up, giving the waves white caps and driving them to crash on the cliffs in bursts of foam that resembled a firework display. On the beaches where tourists gathered, to the north and to the south of the Villa Romana, the sport on such days would change from water skiing to surfboard riding.

The Villa Romana was part of the Duca di Terracini's estate. The ancestral castle stood, an imposing ruin, on the highest point of the immediate coast. Its basilica church of St Francis was still a place of tourist interest, however, as the squat little cherubs flying in the dome just might have been painted by Botticelli. Experts viewed and were divided in this, but in any case it was a pretty little church and worthy of a visit. A previous sinful Duca had caused the church to be desecrated, and there were now no services held in the place.

As the castle became uninhabitable, and the prospect of modernising it too expensive, the last Duca had built

the Villa Romana and walled it in away from the cold
ruin of the castle and the church, both of which were
handed over to the authorities in payment of mounting
taxes. Both were now the property of the Italian version
of the National Trust, and what was left of the castle
had been cemented up and made safe for tourists to view.
Margot had determined to go and view both castle and
church on one of her days off; she was free every Sunday
and from two until five every day; but so far there had
been other things to do and she had no transport. She
hesitated to ask her employers for the use of their car
and was hoping to purchase a bicycle in due course. Although she had heard from Giovanna that a bus went
into Siena twice a day from the road above the villa,
there wasn't much point travelling into Siena on a
Sunday when the shops would all be closed.

There was now, alas, no present Duca di Terracini.
There were various cousins and uncles who were involved in businesses in both Italy and the States. The
villa was occasionally used as a holiday home by a
member of the ancient family who had inherited it as
her share of the estate, but most of the time it was let to
strangers, who had to be rich strangers, obviously, for
the Villa Romana was beautiful and therefore expensive
to run, for inflation had hit Italy in a big way and for
many years.

Margot sometimes wondered what Mr Whitham did
for a living. He was obviously still working even here in
Italy. He drove off to Leghorn daily, and returned hot
and irritable about six, when he took a swim, had a gin
and tonic poured for him, which he sipped by the pool
and would then announce that he was feeling 'civilised'

enough once more to be approachable.

At first Margot had met him at breakfast time, but he was not inclined at that hour to be sociable and made it clear by hiding behind the newspaper as he sipped coffee and saying not a word. Now she took her swim first, and didn't appear in the kitchen until she knew he had left the villa. She was astute enough to realise that he no doubt had problems in his business, whatever it was, and the physical condition of his elder son, which the best of doctors had confirmed as hopeless, in that he would always be paraplegic, had inflicted a deep and ineradicable bruise on his soul.

Whereas men must work, women were allowed to weep, however, and the more Margot got to know Emily Whitham, the more she understood and felt for her. At first she had fancied Mrs Whitham to be hard as nails, brittle and utterly spoilt by her husband. Now she knew, however, that the Whitham family had been blown to smithereens, by the effect of George's accident. They had suffered mental injuries, apparently recovered and grown an armour against unkind fate. The parents pecked unkindly and apparently maliciously at each other, the younger children did the same to each other, only more physically, so that there was always a quarrel going on somewhere, and George was the worst of the lot.

George was almost nineteen, had been an invalid for two years, was beginning to realise that he was helpless and was determined to make everybody pay for it, so that his whole days were devised to bring as much disharmony as possible to those who were nearest and dearest to him and anybody else within his limited reach.

'When he was in hospital,' Mrs Whitham had confided

one day, 'he never would believe it when they said he wouldn't walk again. He said he had feelings in his legs, pains, and that must surely mean they weren't dead and useless. He would lift himself out of bed on his arms —George was always so strong—and fall on the floor. He broke an arm that way. They had to strap him in. Then the talking sessions started. We sent our minister, Mr Campbell, but it was no go. "So let's have some religion, Reverend," George said, "how about a miracle for a start? Have you learnt the bit about *take up thy bed and walk*? Because if you haven't I've got no use for all the rest of what you're saying. Just leave me alone!"

'Then they tried psychiatrists, but George's as sane as you or I, whatever that is. He led them on. He remembered things in his childhood that had never happened and then, next day, would contradict himself and tell quite another story. In a perverted way he enjoyed that part of things, but psychiatrists are busy people and we were told what we already knew, that George would need to come to terms with the situation in his own time. We could have sent him to a sanatorium for people like him, and when we put it to him he said yes, he would like that, to be able to play wheelchair basket-ball and learn to knit with all the other cripples. But he said it in a way which didn't include himself as a cripple.

'If you ask me,' Mrs Whitham said sadly, 'he still thinks this is a temporary situation and so he refuses to accept it as fact. While he's inconvenienced he's going to carry on playing hell. We kept him home, hoping he would settle down and at least allow us to rationalise on the situation as it is and will be. He could still go to university; other paraplegics have; and he's a bright boy. But he has this way of appearing not to listen if he doesn't want to hear, and so far he hasn't wanted to hear. But you must be getting to know him pretty well yourself by now, Nurse,' the voice had taken on a bitter tone. 'Going to give notice soon? I wouldn't blame you. You've stuck it out longer than most.'

'No, I wasn't thinking of going just yet,' Margot said. 'How, exactly, did George's accident happen?'

'He took his father's car. He had met a girl. He was driving an old Ford, but it was off the road. He didn't know this, but we were planning to give him a new car for Christmas, a sports car. So his father said no, he couldn't have his car, and what had happened to legs since his young day? He said that the Ford would soon be repaired and meanwhile George could just hike to his girl-friend's. George argued a bit but John stuck to his guns, and then George seemed to accept the situation and asked if we were going out that evening. "No," I said, "your father and I are planning to watch the film on T.V. But don't be too late back. You need at least eight hours' sleep while you're still at school." John had gone up to shower and when he came downstairs he said he'd better put the car away because stray children could be so mischievous with other people's property. I said not to be long as the T.V. programme was due to start in five minutes, and then he came back with a face like thunder saying the car had gone and he was going to flay George alive when he got home. He'd no sooner said it when the police arrived and they'd found the car in a quarry, and George ...' Here Mrs Whitham had paused and faltered and Margot had asked, softly, about the girl.

'No, thank God he hadn't got to her before it—it happened. We never actually knew who the girl was. She never came to see him in hospital. It isn't that kids aren't caring. It's that they're profoundly embarrassed by it all and don't know what to say. How do you break it to another teenager that his friend is never even going to walk again, let alone go camping and play football? Or to a girl that the boy she met at a disco last week is now a helpless cripple? It's tough, I can tell you. Sometimes I blame myself——'

'How can you say that?' asked Margot.

'Because I don't drive. The children all teased me about it. I just never got up the courage to take lessons and the only time my husband tried to teach me we both finished up nervous wrecks.'

'But I still don't see——?' Margot puzzled.

'Well, if I'd learnt to drive I'd have had my own car, and then George could have taken my car while the Ford was laid up. It's just that John's car was so big and powerful and he had never let George even try it out.'

'The permutations of how or why things happen as they do, or whether they could have been avoided, are endless,' Margot said. 'I think it's best not to look back, for everyone's sake.'

'For one so young you're very wise,' said Emily Whitham. 'How did you get that way?'

'Doing my job, I suppose,' smiled Margot. 'I used to see so many problem cases and became over-involved, at first. I asked myself—or whoever one does ask at such times—why a child of seven was crippled by polio because her parents didn't believe in artificial preventatives, when it was they who deserved to be struck down?

Why the only child of a middle-aged couple, long and lovingly awaited, was a mongol, when the woman in the next bed gave birth to her sixth, and most unwelcome, child, which was normal and healthy in every way? There's no end to the apparent injustices of this world, but I just had to learn to get on with the job and not set myself up as some sort of judge and jury. I think George is a job we all have to get on with, instead of lamenting the fact that he is as he is. You mustn't blame yourself, or anyone.'

This conversation had taken place when they had all been at the Villa Romana a week, and George was being particularly objectionable, mischievous and unhelpful. He had initially resisted everything Margot had to do for and to him, clamping his jaws shut when she needed them open, even once biting the thermometer in two. She had retaliated as calmly as possible by taking his temperature rectally for a couple of times, and since then he had opened his mouth on request, though sulkily.

Bath-times were also a trial. He refused to allow her to bed-bath him, obviously being shy of her youth, though he wouldn't admit this. There was such a storm of protest when she tried to undress him that she allowed him once or twice to wheel himself in a special chair into the shower cubicle, where he performed his own ablutions. One day, however, he had asked, not looking at her, if she would wash his feet.

'I don't seem to be able to reach between my toes,' he had added.

She had done so, gently, and then asked if she might look at him to see that he was properly clean all over.

'No woman is going to——' he began fiercely, but she had silenced him swiftly.

'Now, George, I'm your nurse. I've been a nurse for six years and I've seen all there is to see of the human body, both male and female, and my only concern is with keeping it healthy. Once you understand that I have to do my job, in my way, then we can stop these boring daily arguments.'

'Try and make me,' he invited.

'I will if I have to,' she said promptly. 'I know you're strong. I know that you used to box. But if you won't co-operate with me then I'll call Enrico to hold you still and do what I have to do with him looking on. It's up to you.'

'You—you wouldn't,' he said, at length.

'I not only would but I'm going to call him right now. This absurdity of your outraged modesty has got to stop—with me, at any rate. You're behaving like a shy old maid who finds herself being examined by a male doctor.' She went to ring the nearest bell.

'Wait!' George called, and as she hesitated, 'What do you want to do to me?'

'I've told you,' she answered calmly, 'I want to make sure that you're clean and that your skin is healthy. I want to rub your pressure points.'

'Well then, get on with it. I don't know why you don't give notice or something. All the others did. I get rid of everybody eventually.'

'Should I congratulate you? Well done, George! The patient nobody could stand. Is that what you want to become?'

He scowled. 'You're one of the worst. You're bossy and—ouch, that hurt!'

'I know it did. You have a pressure sore, and that's probably because you haven't dried yourself properly on your own, and the skin has chafed. Perhaps you'll let me bath you in future?'

'Why does it hurt like that? I'm supposed to be paralysed from the waist down.'

'Many paraplegics have pains, unfortunately, in the affected area.'

'Don't call me a paraplegic!'

'It's only a medical condition, not a crime,' soothed Margot.

'But *I'm* not one. They're all mistaken, I tell you. I'll get out of this mess if it's the last thing I do.'

'You can certainly help yourself a great deal. You can exercise and in time become self-reliant. I know a paraplegic woman who eventually went home, ran a house and brought up her daughter with the minimum of outside help. She even dug the garden and grew her own vegetables.'

'Get out!' George said suddenly as she supervised him into his chair. 'Get out! I don't want to hear about stupid cripples who dig gardens! You've done what you wanted to me, so get out!'

'I'm going,' Margot told him. 'You know the way into the garden if you want to go.'

· For a fortnight George threw tantrums, though he never again refused to allow her to care for him professionally. Once he was clean and comfortable, however, he would try one taunt after another until one day he really hit her where it hurt.

'No wonder a girl like you is on the shelf,' he decided. 'Any man with two good legs would run far enough to get away.'

Margot caught her breath and suddenly realised that this was the day Mike and Rose were getting married. She stared back at George until he wriggled.

'What did I say?' he asked. 'You in a trance, or something? Did someone ditch you?'

She blinked her eyes and saw George for what he was at that moment, a hurt creature whose all-consuming instinct was to hurt back, anyhow.

'I'm getting a headache,' she fibbed quietly, 'and if you'll excuse me I'll take something for it.'

George tried other measures when prolonged railing and rudeness availed him little apart from driving everybody away from his vicinity. He awoke one day and didn't say a word. Margot bathed him, helped him dress and got him into his chair and still he didn't speak.

'Lost your tongue, George?' she asked after ascertaining that his pulse and temperature were normal. He merely raised his eyes to the ceiling, as though he had great things to contemplate, and did not respond vocally. All this merely amused Margot, but three hours later his mother was in a panic and sought out the nurse, who was tidying her medicine chest.

'I've sent for Doctor Agostini,' she said. 'George has been struck dumb. Deaf and dumb.'

'Oh, Mrs Whitham! I don't think——'

'Well, you know the way George acts? I've almost got used to it, but he's not speaking and when I talk to him he doesn't hear. I've stood right in front of him and asked if he was O.K. and he just stared at me. Oh, God!'

'Look, Mrs Whitham, I think George is just trying a new trick to gain everybody's attention. There was no need to send for Doctor Agostini. He'll probably be furious. He was only here last Friday.'

'Nurse Walsh, you can't be sure. George was born talking and he hasn't stopped since. He couldn't be quiet if there was a prize for it.'

'George has had a pretty traumatic time these past two years, Mrs Whitham,' Margot reminded her, 'and believe me, such people are capable of anything. It's all part of the trauma.'

Doctor Agostini, a small, hard-worked Italian with a spreadeagled country practice, arrived short-temperedly after leaving his surgery filled with patients, some of whom had travelled miles.

'Well, Nurse, what is wrong?'

'*I* didn't send for you, Doctor. George isn't talking or appearing to hear. Personally I think it's a welcome change, but——'

The doctor gave an understanding little smile and shrugged. 'Well, I will see him.'

George kept silent while he was being examined, though Margot fancied once or twice she saw him smile secretly. The doctor drew Margot to the doorway though he took care they were not out of earshot. 'This is a very serious development, Nurse. I have never seen it before. I must just make sure before I send for specialist. I need to pass a needle through the tongue. Please sedate the patient.' He managed to wink with the eye George couldn't see.

Margot approached George with half an aspirin on a

spoon and a glass of water. He ground his teeth and stared at her.

'Now come on, George,' she mouthed at him clearly. 'This is just to make you sleepy.'

He shook his head, then gaped helplessly as she squeezed his nose and thrust the half tablet down his throat so that he had to swallow. She offered the water, but he was looking past her at Doctor Agostini approaching with what looked like a thick darning needle.

'No!' he shouted suddenly. 'I'm not having that shoved through my tongue. Leave me alone! A guy just feels like a bit of peace and quiet and the Spanish Inquisition is turned loose on him!'

'So you're with us again?' Margot asked, teasingly.

'I can't get away from you, can I?' he demanded. 'Not even when I just want to be alone with my thoughts. I bet you knew all the time and this—this charade was just to scare me. Well, nurse, I'll get even with you. And don't you forget it!'

CHAPTER TWO

GEORGE'S room was on the shady side of the house and Margot threw open the shutters.

'Come on, sleepyhead! Doctor's coming today. Let's get you ready.'

'Grrr!' came the protesting response from the bed.

'Come on now! You can't sleep all day.'

'Why not, for Pete's sake, if I'm tired?'

'Very well, then. You can have a swim, then take breakfast and sleep for the rest of the day. How's that?'

'You're a virago. You know that? O.K. then, pull me up.'

'You can push yourself up. You're a big strong boy.'

'But I'm a tired big strong boy. I'm going back to sleep.'

'George!' Margot reached down and put her arm under his shoulders. 'Now, help a bit.'

Instead she found herself pulled down on top of him and held as in a vice. George's blue eyes regarded her assessingly and his teeth gleamed in a gleeful smile.

'What are you going to do now?' George asked. 'How about a little kiss?'

Margot had not nursed for six years without learning a few tricks, however. She could remember Sister Tutor's words, now, as though she had heard them only yesterday. 'When you nurse *men*, nurses, you will find that at times they will treat you as sexual objects. These are the ones who are well enough to be awaiting discharge, and those coming round from anaesthetics who are confused and may imagine you are their wives.' Here a giggle had gone round the classroom, frowned into silence by the authority on the daís. 'There's no need to be a black-belt judo expert. You just need to know a few simple tricks to tackle such situations.'

Margot tried one of them now, and George released his hold and caught his breath in shocked surprise. He even sat up on the rebound.

'I'm sorry about that, George, but you're not to try anything like that again,' said Margot calmly.

'It was only a bit of fun,' he growled, obviously feeling a little embarrassed now.

'It wasn't funny for me,' she told him. 'You may find this difficult to believe, but I prize my dignity, and that scene wasn't very dignified. Supposing somebody had come in?'

He allowed her to take off his pyjamas and put his swimming trunks on. All the while she was trying not to show her inner nervousness, for now she knew that George was a young man with all a man's instincts, and he had made her feel young and vulnerable and female for that split second before she had used her knee to break his stranglehold on her. She could not afford that George should regard her as a sexual object: he was doomed to grow into his manhood's emotions with enough handicaps as it was.

In a kind of troubled silence she put his bathrobe round him, helped him into his chair and wheeled him off down the garden towards the swimming pool, calling Enrico, the handyman and chauffeur, as she went. Enrico was tall for an Italian, and he was famous in the nearby village for his wrestling prowess. Like Salvatore and Giovanna he went with the villa, and could tackle most of the domestic problems, including the plumbing, when he was not required to drive the car. When Mrs Whitham needed to go shopping in Siena, he was instructed to hire a car and drive her, but mostly the family stayed in or near the villa.

It was difficult to travel with George, who needed his chair with him, and though he hated to be bundled into cars he created his own brand of hell when it was suggested he stay behind. It was easier to put up with George in comparative privacy than allow him to rail in public, and as all produce was delivered to the villa, including fruit and vegetables which Giovanna bought fresh daily, from an old man who carried his goods in panniers on an equally ancient donkey, there was really no need to go far afield often.

George had been having swimming therapy for a week, on Doctor Agostini's orders. He had once been a fine swimmer and could use his arms to advantage. Enrico carried him like a baby into the shallow end of the pool, though George, even now, must have weighed eleven and a half stone, and the boy would haul himself on his powerful arms to and fro the breadth of the pool, his useless limbs dragging behind him. Now he spoke to Enrico in Italian and the big fellow went off.

'Why have you sent him away?' Margot asked. 'I can't get you out of there on my own, you know.'

'I told him to come back in half an hour. I mean to work up a real good appetite.'

He swam to and fro, to and fro. Margot was very pleased with him and even softened a little towards him personally. If he enjoyed swimming so much, why shouldn't he be allowed extra time in the pool? She perched on one of the stone benches beside the pool, felt the sun warm on her face and closed her eyes. When she opened them she saw George swimming strongly the length of the pool, which was about twenty yards long and over ten feet deep at the far end.

'George!' she shouted, running along the edge. 'You're not supposed to swim down there. You promised Doctor Agostini you wouldn't take risks. Come back to the shallow end at once!'

'Fuss, fuss! I can swim, can't I?' He touched the rail at the deep end and turned as though to swim back. 'You realise that water's more buoyant the deeper it is?' He seemed to be standing upright, as though treading water to illustrate, but she knew that George couldn't tread water. His legs were useless. While she watched he slid down below the surface. A few bubbles came up, but when she looked again the figure of George was prone on the bottom in ten feet of water.

'Enrico! Salvatore!' she shrieked, and kicking off her shoes took a header into the pool. Diving was not her greatest achievement. It took three attempts, hampered as she was by her wet overall, to grab hold of George and tow him to the surface. Somehow she managed to keep both their heads above water and struggled to the shallow end. She was gasping with exhaustion, half-tearful and thankful to find that both Enrico and Salvatore had appeared to relieve her of her burden.

She managed to indicate that George be laid on his stomach, his head on one side, and showed Enrico how to help her by pressing hard on the muscular young back. No water came out of George's mouth, however, and she put her ear anxiously to his face.

'Oh, my God, he's not breathing!' she said with a whimper, and turned George over. She indicated that Enrico should hold the boy's head still and, taking air into her own lungs, opened George's mouth, pinched his nostrils and breathed air into him.

After several similar efforts she fancied his chest rose and fell, but it stilled again almost immediately. She was about to recommence the mouth-to-mouth resuscitation when there was a sound. It was like stifled laughter.

Margot was about to tell her helpers that this was a nice time to chuckle, though they wouldn't have understood her, when she looked down into George's laughing blue eyes. He took one glance at her anxious, tear-stained face, her soaking hair and overall, and let out a loud laugh, rolling about on the edge of the pool like one possessed.

'You made all that up?' she asked fiercely. 'You mean to say you faked the whole thing?'

'I didn't fake anything,' he chuckled. 'It was your show. You wanted to play the heroine. I've always been able to hold my breath under water for longer than most people. I was just checking that I could still do it. Then there you were, up and down in the water like a yo-yo and hauling me along. It was fun.'

'But you stopped breathing,' Margot said, still not quite believing it had all been an act.

'I know. Every time you checked I held my breath. And it paid off'—he laughed at her—'I got my kiss.'

'Oh, you! You!' Margot was so angry and uncomfortable that she scarcely knew what to do. She stormed off towards the house, weeping with fury, not exactly in the mood to meet a perfect stranger and be civil to him.

The stranger was tall, and very brown. He wore a red chequered shirt, a pair of old, unpressed slacks and a rakish panama hat.

'Not today,' Margot snapped, 'and you shouldn't be in here. This is private property.' She walked on.

'Just a minute!' came after her, so that she whirled around and saw that in the brown face were a pair of stormy steely blue eyes. 'How can you be sure you don't want my product until you know what it is?'

'Because we don't buy at the door,' Margot returned. 'Only Giovanna does that, and at the *back* door.'

She suddenly realised that they were conversing in English. This stranger was as English as she was, and she was soaking wet and angry and must be creating a terrible impression.

'If you're an artist, or anything like that,' she proceeded, 'then you're wasting your time. The family isn't up yet and they *do not buy* from casual callers.'

'How wise!' said the stranger, tipping his hat a little more rakishly. He looked beyond her to where George, still in fits of laughter, was being lifted into his chair by Enrico.

'Is that the patient?' he asked. 'Doctor Agostini's patient?'

'Are you a doctor?' Margot asked, looking him up and down disbelievingly.

'No, I'm a parachutist. You'd better get out of those wet things, Nurse whatever-your-name-is, and I'll see you later. I should take your dip more fittingly attired, if I were you. Agostini told me you were very sensible, but I shall make up my own mind on that score when I know you better. The name's Massey—Guy Massey. You can call me Doctor or not, as you wish. I'm not a stickler for protocol.'

As Margot changed into dry underclothes and a fresh white overall, she felt utterly and miserably wronged by her own hasty and hysterical behaviour. Not about saving George, for had the emergency been genuine then haste was necessary, but about her head-on collision with the strange English doctor who must have decided she was every kind of a spoilt brat. Even had he been a casual hawker she had no right to vent her spleen on him, and knew she would have regretted her behaviour almost immediately, but to speak like that to a doctor was unforgivable and indefensible. In hospital she had never, to her knowledge, allowed her irritation to show to a member of the medical staff, even when they sometimes contradicted themselves within minutes, or allowed themselves public displays of vituperation against herself or a nursing colleague. It was hammered into nurses from their first arrival at Preliminary Training School that doctors, as a breed, were sacrosanct, and Ward Sisters only one degree less so. There were girls who were normally extrovert, who would occasionally try it on and answer back, but doctors were past masters in the art of quelling insubordination, and also had the satisfaction of knowing that Sister would take over where they had left off. No nurse was allowed to be cheeky twice.

'What must he think of me?' Margot asked as she combed damp hair smooth. 'I don't know how I'm going to look him in the face again.'

She heard laughter coming from the shaded terrace where George was sitting, dressed now in shirt and shorts, which he had obviously donned himself or perhaps with assistance from Enrico. Doctor Massey was perched on a stone lion and the two were obviously sharing a joke. Margot felt it must be about her, as silence fell at her appearance.

'We don't need you just now, Nurse,' the doctor said without looking at her. 'I'm sure you've got other things to do?'

'Yes, sir,' she decided to respond, and even that

sounded impertinent in her own ears as she turned on her heels and went to fiddle about in George's room, picking up his wet trunks from the floor and rinsing them out automatically before putting them in a warm cabinet to dry.

She had not been quite so miserable since she had heard of Mike's defection, coming, as it had done, on the heels of her mother's death. There was something about Doctor Massey's steel-blue glance which had cut her like a knife; it had injured her professional integrity, to which she had clung as a lifeline during her emotional unhappiness. She now wondered if she was right to stay on with George, questioning if she was really here for his sake or her own. It seemed to her that the English doctor had asked the same thing, and was prepared to bide his time before deciding. All sorts of doubts now clouded her horizon, which only this morning had appeared so settled and clear.

She heard Mrs Whitham descend the stairs calling for coffee, and then the other children, Tessa and Van, hurtled down and screamed at each other as they headed for the pool.

'You're not coming in with me, you little pig!'

'Try and stop me, *and* Oscar's coming too.'

Oscar was probably Van's pet toad or snake. He had quite a collection of wild things gathered from the surrounding hills and dried-out river-bed.

Margot tidied her own room unnecessarily, for a local girl came in to clean regularly, and though she could hear the members of the family now on the terrace, and Doctor Massey's dark brown voice, and she could smell fragrant coffee, pride made her keep away from the gathering. Normally she would have rubbed George's pressure points half an hour ago, but she had been dismissed, and dismissed she would stay while *he* was present.

Twenty minutes later Emily Whitham sought her out.

'Oh, Nurse, I'm sorry about that trick George played on you. It must have upset you at the time.'

'Everybody else seems to have found it side-splitting,' Margot said, a little acidly.

'Oh, you *are* upset.'

Margot immediately thawed. 'I'll probably see the funny side of it later,' she smiled, 'but my reaction was to give Doctor Massey the rough edge of my tongue. I didn't know he was a doctor, of course.'

'Oh, that reminds me,' Mrs Whitham exclaimed, 'he wants to see you. He's in the main hall and thought you'd perhaps walk up to the gate with him. A very charming man. It appears he's going to be looking after George from now on.'

'I see.' Margot automatically straightened her overall and went towards the red and white tessellated entrance hall of the villa, which opened on to a wide porch and twin curls of stone, balustraded steps leading down to a gravelled driveway. George was never brought out this way because of the steps and Margot sometimes forgot that the handsome entrance to the villa existed.

Doctor Massey was down on his knees with his old panama hat laid aside. At first Margot thought he was praying and held back, but then she told herself that she was in a mood to expect the ridiculous today, and announced herself.

'Yes, Doctor? You wanted to see me?'

He didn't look up. He said, 'I do believe that's an Etruscan tile. It could be the genuine article just shoved in among the rest. Take a look.'

Margot knelt also, and saw a cracked tile showing a warrior in a blue chariot.

'I don't know anything about antiquities,' she said. 'Could it be—what you said?'

'I'm studying the Etruscan period,' he told her. 'They had tiles in their bath houses just like that.'

'How interesting!' she commented. 'I'm sorry I was so rude to you earlier,' she added quickly, 'I wasn't to know you were a doctor.'

'And if I hadn't been a doctor it would have been all right, would it?' He was still studying the tile and didn't see the way she flushed.

'I didn't mean that,' she said heatedly. 'I was in a mood, I suppose, to be rude to anyone.'

'Yes, you were in quite a state,' he agreed, and stood up. 'Come on, walk with me up to the front gate.'

He did not speak until they had passed through the wrought-iron gates and he had tossed a couple of coins to a small ragamuffin boy who had obviously been in charge of the dusty red Alfa Romeo open tourer. The child ran off shouting *'Grazie, dottore!'* and then he leaned against the car and regarded her.

'Is George getting you down?' he asked.

She gave him a swift glance.

'I suppose he is,' she replied. 'He and—and other things.'

'Was it the "other things" which made you take George on in the first place?'

'You have no right——!' she flared, then she lowered

her eyes. 'I had certain private reasons for coming out here,' she said. 'I lost my mother, for one thing.'

'Oh, I'm sorry. But that was only one of the reasons, I take it?'

'Look, Doctor, I'm not your patient. Have the Whithams been complaining about me?'

'On the contrary, they think you're the cat's pyjamas. They're afraid George might succeed in driving you away, and in his own way I do believe George himself is rather attached to you.'

'He was certainly attached to me this morning,' Margot answered wryly. 'We had quite a wrestling match on his bed. He's surprisingly strong. I had to——' she bit her lip and looked out across the distant dry hills. 'Then the swimming pool episode on top of it! You'll all have had a good laugh about that. The way I jumped in, as I was, and dragged him out and then gave him the kiss of life——' She looked at Doctor Massey and saw a twinkling pair of very blue eyes regarding her.

'Full marks to George for initiative,' he chuckled. 'But I wouldn't take that business too seriously. It's really very funny when you think about it.'

'Funny? I was out of my mind with worry. I was telling one of the Italians to phone for an ambulance, but they don't understand English.'

'No, the Italian peasant is not noted for his linguistic ability, but they were telling me that they tried to tell you George was O.K., that he was only playing a game, but that you wouldn't listen.'

She looked at him only half-comprehendingly.

'You mean they *knew*, and I was going through the

whole routine of resuscitation? What an idiot they must think I am!'

'You *could* learn Italian,' he suggested. 'It's quite easy.'

'I'm quite busy, you know. George is quite a handful.'

'But you have time off?'

'I have a free day on Sunday.'

'You don't seem to have been anywhere since you came here,' he observed. 'Doctor Agostini has never seen you in the village or down on the beach. *I've* never seen you, and I live in a small villa not ten minutes away. I think you've shut yourself up here with a secret sorrow and believe if you keep the world out you won't get hurt again. That's wrong. You have to come out from hiding and take anything that's coming to you.'

She forced a wry smile. 'Are you a trained psychiatrist, Doctor?'

'No. I'm an orthopaedic surgeon who smashed his operating hand in an accident and became a casualty instead. I do know a bit about creeping away and hiding— I did it. I came here and pretended to be an amateur archaeologist. It was only when the village was laid low by an outbreak of typhus that I surfaced and realised that I couldn't escape from doing my real job. Agostini, who's near to retirement age, couldn't cope with the situation on his own—his two sons have gone to work in smart clinics, one in Rome and the other in New York—and so I picked up my battered black bag and volunteered as a G.P., and now I'm in partnership with Agostini. He's asked me to take George over, and so here I am. Now, what's your story? Why are you here?'

'I told you, I lost my mother.'

'But not your job, surely?' he probed. 'Nurses are in great demand in England, even though they still get paid in peanuts.'

'I just wanted to get away for a while. I felt a bit aggressive at the time and fancied I could take George on.'

'And now you're not feeling so aggressive, eh?' the doctor enquired. 'Whatever made you good and mad back home you've either forgotten or forgiven. But that's no reason why you should stagnate. I don't want George's nurse as a patient too. I'm going to give you some good advice and you can take it or not as you please. Firstly you're going to see Mrs Whitham and tell her you want Thursdays off instead of Sundays. Thursdays I'm free, and I can give you an outing occasionally. Also I'm not after anything. Our association would be purely platonic, and if you met Mr Wonderful I'd drop out of the picture quite gracefully. Secondly, there's an odd old Scots lady who gives Italian lessons by arrangement at the Villa Montefiore along the cliff road. That would add to your education, give you an interest and enable you to understand the servants, and also hear what young George is saying to them.'

He smiled. 'Doctor's orders are that you start getting out and about, as of now. Understand?'

'I understand,' agreed Margot. 'But you're obviously an extremely self-sufficient person and won't want me tagging along every Thursday indefinitely. Mr Wonderful just might not turn up and I should hate to be a bore, or have you feeling obligated.'

'Right. So we'll keep the option open for a month and then discuss it again. I'll see you Thursday next, at nine-thirty, and we'll go into Siena. There's a very good museum there, and a *trattoria* where the pizzas are out of this world.' He was scribbling on a note-pad and she noticed that he wrote with his left hand. His right hand appeared stiff, the middle and third fingers rigid. 'That's Miss MacDougal's address. Thanks for seeing me out. *Arrivederci!*'

She watched the red car disappear in a cloud of dust feeling vaguely disorientated. He was the sort of man who seemed to take one over, dictate to one, and—if one was not careful—to whom one submitted. Well, she was prepared to admit it was time she left the villa and explored the world beyond its walls, but she wasn't prepared to say 'Yes sir, no sir, three bags full, sir', to anyone.

Yes, she was prepared to accept Guy Massey's offer as escort until she became accustomed to going out and about on her own, and she *would* take Italian lessons. Why not? A new language was like growing a new limb, it became an extra prop. And how dared he tell her their acquaintance would be merely platonic, as though in his time nurses in their hundreds had fallen madly in love with him in a one-sided way? Oh, yes, he was good-looking, but he wasn't the answer to every maiden's prayer by any means. Why, she didn't even know if he was married or engaged—and come to that, she didn't even care. She would go out with him once or twice and then tell him that she really didn't need his escort any more.

She rehearsed the scene all the way back to the house even to the point where she envisaged his countenance dropping, then looking positively chagrined. A smile broke upon her lips so that when she saw George he thought it was on account of him, that he was, in fact, forgiven.

'Nurse!' he said when he saw her. 'I thought you were really mad at me and that you were sulking. I can't stand people who sulk.'

'I *was* mad at you,' she told him, 'but I haven't been sulking. I've been talking to Doctor Massey. Where did you learn Italian?' she asked.

'We've been coming here every summer since I can remember. Not always to this villa, of course. I suppose I picked it up. Why?'

'Because I'm going to have lessons and then I'll know what you're telling the servants in future,' replied Margot. 'If you have so much energy for making mischief I don't know why you can't continue your studies. Weren't you planning to be a lawyer?'

'Yes, I was,' he said gloomily, 'but I don't see myself going to law school in a wheelchair.'

'I don't see why not. Your brain isn't affected, George.'

'Now look here,' he said viciously, 'I get enough of that rubbish about pulling myself together and coming to terms with living from my dad. I'm not taking it from you, see? You just do your job and shut up about cripples leading normal lives.' He leaned deliberately and knocked over a jug of lemon juice from the table by his side. 'Bring me some fresh lemon,' he demanded.

'Sorry, it's not my job to look after a spoilt child. When you've grown up a bit I'll be back. In the meanwhile, if you're thirsty, you can get along to the tap.'

'Hey, you——!' A piece of the broken jug hit the lintel of the door behind her and she withdrew just far enough to observe what George would do next. He looked down at the pieces of broken jug, then at his hands, which he clenched and unclenched until at length he put them up to cover his eyes for a moment. Margot's instinct was to rush out and comfort him, but she knew George would never forgive her for seeing him in a weak moment.

When he was himself again she went out and said clearly, 'I haven't brought you more lemonade because I believe lunch is ready. Come on. After lunch you can have a nice nap. You were very tired this morning, as I remember.'

Mrs Whitham was quite amenable to Margot's changing her day off.

'When we first came you didn't seem too bothered about going out,' she said, 'and it was easier for me to have John home when you weren't around. But of course you can take Thursdays off in future. Doctor Massey did say you needed to get right away from George occasionally, and I had to agree. I suppose I'd got used to the idea that you didn't mind him too much, and he seemed to have settled down to the idea of having you around. But this morning's performance proved that George has never really settled. It's just that the pauses seem to be getting longer between his outbreaks.'

She hesitated. 'I was really afraid that you would want to leave us when I heard what he'd done to you, and John insists we're not going to keep on hiring new nurses who stick it for a week or two and then make off. He says George goes into a sanatorium when you leave us. He's not prepared to have the rest of the family sacrificed for him. John has been patient, but this family trouble is taking toll of us all. I have no patience to spare for Tessa, who's reaching the age when she needs her mother most, or with Van, who reminds me so much of George at his age. And John and I—we have our problems——'

Margot said impulsively, 'Don't worry, Mrs Whitham, I'm not going to leave George if you really think I can help him. What he did today has made me just that much wiser. I'll be watching out in future. If it helps you at all, your family's trouble has helped me to forget mine. When I first took George on I was full of woes, and the physical challenge he presented gave me no time to wallow. Now I think I'm emerging from that bad time, and I sincerely hope and pray that, with time, you'll emerge from yours. I'll help all I can. I think, in a way, George likes me,' she added cheerfully. 'Earlier today he practically apologised to me, as though he was afraid he'd gone too far. He's always telling me he wishes I would go like all the rest, but I do get the feeling he doesn't really mean it. Now I'd better go and help him into bed.'

CHAPTER THREE

THE first Thursday Margot was to meet Guy Massey, she was disappointed when she awoke and discovered the day was overcast. She had promised Mrs Whitham that she would get George up and stay until the woman was downstairs to take over. It was Tessa who arrived, however, wearing a towelling robe and in bare feet.

'Mother says you're to go, Nurse. She'll be down in a

minute, but I'm taking George for his swim.'

'Like hell you are!' he retorted promptly. 'No little sister of mine is doing anything for me. I can take myself for my swim.'

He pushed himself off through the open french windows and down the garden walk. Tessa looked hurt and helpless. Tears glinted behind her long lashes.

'Go on after him,' Margot encouraged. 'Don't force yourself on him, just take your own swim as though he wasn't there. There's always Enrico to help him.'

'But I want to be a nurse. I think it's a wonderful profession. But if I can't even help my own brother ...'

'Don't be put off nursing because of George,' encouraged Margot. 'Actually he's not really ill, you know.' Tessa looked at her with startled, wide blue eyes.

'The physical injuries have healed, as far as they're going to,' Margot explained, 'and you could do my job here easily, if it wasn't for the fact that I don't think he'd accept a member of his family as his nurse. It's the mental blockage we're dealing with, and that means letting him get on with things in his own way and not showing how he can hurt you, until he comes to terms with himself. George is fighting a long, lonely battle and if other people get in the way they'll get hurt. Try to carry on as though everything was normal, Tessa. I know it's difficult, but then nothing worth doing is ever easy. I must go now. I'll see you this evening.'

The red Alfa Romeo was gleaming. A youth gave a final loving polish to its bonnet as Margot arrived at the Villa Fiorita, which was really just two old cottages joined together. They were whitewashed and had strange curly orange brown tiles on the roof, a couple of which were missing. There was no garden in front, but an old walled compound stretched out behind and scents of undetected blossoms came pungently to her nostrils. The front door, which was really two doors knocked into one, stood open, and as Margot knocked a hen scuttered out with a loud squawking and lost a few downy feathers in the process. A woman's voice called out sleepily,

'Darling, I think there's someone at the door. I thought you'd made it clear patients weren't to come here!'

Margot grew rigid, and was about to tiptoe away when *his* voice spoke, and she whirled around to see him wiping the last of the lather from his handsome face.

'It's all right, Maxine, it's not a patient. I won't be a minute, Nurse Walsh. Would you like a cup of coffee?'

'No, thanks. I've had breakfast,' she said rigidly. 'Don't hurry over your own.'

This time she turned right away, thinking, 'So he's married? And she doesn't seem to mind if he goes off with other women on his day off? Well, it's no business of mine.'

She heard him ask the woman, Maxine, if she wanted anything from Siena, and he came out carrying a list which he tucked into his bush-type shirt pocket; the shirt looked decidedly faded and so were his denims. If it hadn't been for the car she would have imagined him to be poor.

They had driven about ten kilometres when Guy Massey said suddenly, without looking at her, 'It's always a shock seeing a nurse out of uniform. I scarcely recognised you just now. Fortunately I'd remembered your eyes.'

She scarcely knew how to take this and laughed uneasily.

'Just how many girls were you expecting at your house at half-past nine?' she asked. 'Surely you didn't have to look at my eyes to remember that you offered to accompany me today?'

He didn't answer the first part of her question but said, 'Oh, I always look at eyes. In my youth I used to have dates with girls who were either knock-kneed or bandy, simply because they had nice eyes.'

Margot wondered furiously what he had decided about her eyes.

'Ah, happy, carefree youth!' he exclaimed nostalgically. 'We discover all too soon that there's more to a woman than her anatomy.'

'Thank goodness for that! We women make a few discoveries, too,' she retorted.

He drove another ten kilometres, then spoke again.

'That's a very auspicious beginning to our acquaintance, Miss Walsh! On our first meeting you flew at me like a harpy with storm-clouds in your grey eyes, and now here we are merely sheathing the daggers in our words. We're already well on the way to hating one another. Interesting.'

'I don't intend to hate you, Doctor Massey, because that would make you feel important, and your sense of self-importance is outsize already. I didn't ask to come out with you, but since I have, I have also no intention of pandering to your masculine vanity.'

'Back to your corner, Champ, the round's over,' he mocked. 'I wonder whom you're really fighting?' he asked, as though to himself. 'Because this isn't the beginning of the battle. I have stepped in like a punch-ball, haven't I? Is it the whole of mankind or one in particular who socked you so hard it's made you mad? No, don't answer! I had no right to ask.'

He overtook an old man on a mule with a herd of goats. The car went perilously near to the edge of an unguarded drop and Margot closed her eyes until they were safely speeding onwards again.

He whistled, slightly off-key, so that she decided he was merely doing it to irritate her, but the grey cloud that had obscured the morning was now lifting and letting the sun filter through. Soon she was feeling elated and watched the unfolding landscape with interest.

'That was the tail-end of a sandstorm from Africa,' her companion suddenly volunteered.

'What was?'

'The grey pall that has spattered your pretty white dress and put smuts on your nose.'

She couldn't see any spattering on her dress and opened her handbag to look in her mirror. Her nose was short, slightly tilted and quite clean.

'There you go again!' she said with a sigh. 'I'm not surprised your wife is glad to see the back of you for a bit.'

'My wife glad——?' he questioned.

'Maxine, I think you called her?'

'Oh,' he changed a gear to pull them up a steep haul, 'Maxine. Yes, I'm sure she's glad to have me out of the way. I affect most women like that in time.'

'Do you really wonder?'

'You're an unkind little harpy, aren't you?' he asked her. 'A female porcupine. Perhaps I was wrong to let you out of that luxurious gaol of yours. Why do you want to fight me?'

'I'm not aware that I do. It's just that you rub me up the wrong way all the time.'

'I can see our acquaintance, apart from the professional side of it, is not going to last more than the statutory month we decided.'

'*You* decided,' she corrected. 'It's you who made sweeping statements like us keeping the option open for a month.'

'What was wrong with that?' he enquired.

'I don't like the idea of anybody feeling sorry for me. I'm a very self-sufficient person, actually.'

'Lucky you! Well, now that we're coming into Siena do you want to go off on your own?'

'I have some shopping to do,' she said, rather shortly, as he found a parking place.

'So have I, for Maxine, mostly,' Guy patted his breast pocket. 'Well, the museum isn't hard to find if you want to look me up, but I'll understand if your self-sufficiency takes over. See you later.'

She tried not to let him see she had to follow him on the short cut to the centre of the town, but then she quickly lost him. She hadn't thought Siena would be so bustling; there were positive crowds in the market place and a plethora of brilliantly hued flowers, fruits and vegetables. A silversmith was beating out the charms of the Zodiac, but she passed on as soon as he began to pester her to buy. She wasn't intending shopping for souvenirs on this occasion. She wanted things like soap and toothpaste and cool, scanty cotton underwear for the hotter days ahead.

She eventually found the equivalent of an English draper's shop, though the undies it sold varied from the positively saucy to the more utilitarian Italian mammas' garments, so Margot settled for a couple of pairs of sheer black tights and a bra. Even so these were much more expensive than she had thought, or else the price had gone up as her English accent was noted. She proceeded on into the town to find a chemist's shop, and here, fortunately, everything was marked, so that she could not be cheated. Having completed her shopping she set out to explore Siena, noting the tiers of reddish-brown roofs which must surely account for that name in any child's paintbox, Burnt Sienna. She wandered around for about an hour, felt thirsty and indulged in a coffee at a pavement café.

'It can't be!' she groaned at the price even of that. Of course she had been warned; coffee on the continent, though excellent, was an expensive luxury and it was cheaper to drink the local wine. She walked on, away from the shopping area so as not to be tempted to buy anything, and headed for a nearby church, hesitating when she saw a one-legged beggar on the steps.

'I shouldn't,' she told herself. 'He probably has a perfectly good artificial limb he finds it more profitable not to wear.'

'But supposing he hasn't ...?' she thought the very next moment, and parted with more lire than she could afford simply because she hadn't any small change.

The church was baroque and very colourful, with gilded cherubs supporting the domed roof and statues of the Virgin, clad in brilliant blues.

'I do feel a bit lonely,' Margot admitted to herself as

she sat in a pew and regarded the intricately-carved reredos behind the flower-drenched altar. She felt she couldn't lie, even to herself, in church. 'I suppose I'll make friends eventually, and then it will all be more fun to be out and about.'

An old woman, all in black, came in, made her devotions and lit a candle. She then espied Margot, looked at her pointedly and obviously scolded her soundly. It was probably because the visitor's head was uncovered.

'Scusi, scusi!' Margot said, rising, and beholding a side exit to the church made her departure.

'Even driven out of church!' she muttered self-pityingly.

The street she was in was short and dark and narrow. She was now feeling decidedly hungry and looked in her purse to see how much she could afford for lunch. A trattoria, she remembered, would be cheaper than a ristorante, unless she was again taken for a ride. She replaced her purse in her handbag and then stood back as a youth on a noisy scooter came towards her. The next moment, to her horror and disbelief, he was tugging at her handbag and accelerating away.

'Help!' she cried as she was dragged along, then she had to let go and fell flat into the roadway, taking fouled dust into her nostrils and tasting blood on her lips.

The old woman of the church episode appeared and tut-tutted as she pulled Margot to her feet.

'I've been robbed!' the girl shouted, and pointed after the scooter which had disappeared round the next bend into a main street.

The beggar hopped up. He and the old woman dusted Margot down and spoke rapidly to one another.

'Don't you understand?' Margot asked. 'He stole my handbag.' She indicated her empty hands, but one was grazed and the old woman promptly spat on it and rubbed it.

'Leave me alone!' Margot shouted, wiping the hand on her dress. 'I want the police. *Polizia!*' she repeated.

Hearing this dreaded word the beggar hopped backwards, his pockets jingling with the effort, and then turned and made his way off, looking over his shoulder at intervals. The old woman, too, raised her shoulders in a shrug as though deciding the *signorina* was an ungrateful dead loss and waddled away. Margot wanted to cry with fright and frustration, but she remembered seeing a street-sign on her journey here.

She retraced her steps, trying not to look conspicuous with her dress soiled, a hole in the right knee of her tights, a bloody lip and hand and maybe a burst nose. She couldn't be sure what sort of a wreck she looked as she had no mirror to consult.

As she entered the museum reaction was setting in, and she was cold and trembling even though her brow was damp with sweat. She made her way through various galleries and almost fell into the Etruscan room. Guy Massey was the only person there and looked up in amazement at the vision she presented.

'Oh, dear!' she wailed. 'I didn't want to be a nuisance, but I'm afraid I've had a little accident. I—I do feel odd.'

All at once his arms were round her and she was weeping against his broad chest, with a hint of coal-tar soap about it. She left a soggy patch of tear-stain on him and a few streaks of blood, and then she gave an odd apologetic little laugh which was merely an extension of the tears.

'Here!' he put the neck of a small bottle to her lips. 'Have a good swig. Medical comforts,' he smiled. 'I never travel without it.'

The brandy made her feel warmer but even odder, so that this time she fell willingly into his arms. He held her comfortingly and she clung on to him a good time longer than was necessary. She felt like a little ship which has been driven and battered by storm winds and finds itself safely in harbour at last. Reluctantly she pushed herself away from him apologetically.

'I expect I'll live,' she said, not looking at him.

'What happened, exactly?'

'I had my handbag stolen,' she explained, 'a boy on a moped. He just pulled me over and I had to let go.'

'How much did you lose? Anything important?'

'It was all-important to me. All my things. Not much money—about ten English pounds' worth of lire.'

'I mean, were you carrying your passport or a credit card?'

'No. My passport's in my trunk and I haven't got a credit card.'

'Then it's all replaceable stuff? I mean, the things women cram into their handbags, combs and compacts and lipsticks and such trivia?'

'Yes,' Margot said. She didn't add that there had also been an irreplaceable snapshot of Mike and herself taken in bygone happy days.

'Come on!' Guy spoke briskly. 'We've got to get you cleaned up a bit, and then we'll go to the police and make all the correct noises. You won't get your money back, but you just might get the bag.'

He escorted her to a door marked *'Signore'* and spoke to a woman in charge of the place in fluent Italian. Margot found herself being bathed tenderly the while the woman ranted about the scum of her countryfolk. At last Margot came out looking and feeling decidedly better, though she was still very pale and had the blue shadows of recent shock below her eyes. Guy Massey put his hand firmly under her elbow and propelled her from the museum, down the steps and along the nearby street.

'It's not far to the police station,' he said. 'Then you're going to have lunch. Everything looks better on a full stomach.'

Margot was a mere, rather confused onlooker as her companion spoke to the desk sergeant in the police station. It seemed to her that the Italian policeman spoke with everything he possessed; his voice was active, but so were his arms and his shoulders, his eyes and his eyebrows, which did an eloquent dance of their own.

'Come on!' said Guy, and they were shown into the Chief of Police's office. He was beautifully uniformed and looked languid, but here also the eyes and eyebrows joined in with his speech, and his shoulders seemed to be permanently raised as his hands performed their own graceful pas de deux.

'He says,' explained Guy Massey, 'that it's probably a student at work. Whenever the universities are closed for vacations, something like this occurs. He's going to see if anything has been handed in this morning.'

An untidy, harassed-looking policeman came in with an armful of handbags, which he dropped in front of the captain. Margot recognised her own immediately. The strap was broken and when she opened it there were no contents.

'They empty them when they're brought in,' Guy explained. 'Can you list the contents, apart from the money, that is? I doubt you'll get that back.'

'I want to get out of here,' Margot suddenly declared. 'I feel sick.'

'What about your bag?'

'I never want to see it again. Let me get out!'

Guy Massey rejoined her on the street and told her to breathe deeply.

'I had to thank all concerned,' he said rather reproachfully. 'Why did you let me start all that business if you didn't want the damned thing back after all?'

'I don't know,' she answered helplessly, 'I'm sorry. I feel contaminated by it all. I—I hate this place.'

'Don't be ridiculous. People are getting their pockets picked all the time in London, but you wouldn't say you hated London, would you?'

'No, of course not. I apologise for being so stupid and naïve. Nothing like that has ever happened to me before, and I suppose it's always a shock the first time. It even makes me wonder about the old woman in the church, and the cripple——'

She told him the whole story.

'Oh, I'm sure they weren't involved in any way,' he rejoined. 'Probably they never even knew you'd been robbed but just thought you'd hurt yourself. Italians are very soft-hearted. When you mentioned the police, of course the beggar moved on. They're trying to clean up the cities of such people. All this goes to prove that you must learn the language. Have you done anything yet, about Miss MacDougal?'

'Yes, I'm having my first lesson tomorrow at four o'clock. I must admit that not being able to speak to anyone made the experience doubly frightening. But I mustn't be a bore. I'm ruining your day off with my troubles.'

'Let's go the that *pizzeria* I told you about. The shops are closed now, and we can dally over lunch. Later you can help me with Maxine's list'—he patted his pocket to make sure the folded paper was still there—'and we'll buy you a new handbag and so on. No, I insist. You can pay me back when convenient.'

A little colour stole back into Margot's cheeks as she ate the pizza he had ordered for her, which came up to all his eulogies of it, and sipped a glass of Chianti. They talked shop for a little while, comparing notes of hospitals where they had worked in the past, and then the talk came round to hospital romances.

'They can be utterly disastrous if carried to conclusion,' Guy Massey opined. 'Supposing a riveter in a shipyard married a woman riveter, if there were such people, and all they had to talk about was riveting when they got home at night?'

Margot was laughing as she finished her pizza.

'And you think hospital personnel, if they married, would only talk about hospitals?'

'In the main, yes. It would be artificial of them not to. But I think on the whole it's better to get right away from the atmosphere of one's job when one isn't occupied doing it.'

'I take it that Mrs Massey was not a doctor or a nurse?'

He looked at her sharply.

'No, she was not.'

'So. Then you've proved your point.'

'Would you like an ice?' he asked. 'I can recommend them here. Luigi——!' he called.

'*Si, signor.*'

As she started on her mound of ice-cream, Margot decided that she had been practically told to keep off the grass regarding his marriage. Maybe he had secret regrets that he was unable to find some common ground for conversation with his wife, be it riveting or the wider world of hospitals and medicine.

When at last they finished an excellent meal with cups of coffee, she asked, 'Does your hand pain you at all?'

'No.' He looked at his stiff fingers. 'Not any more. Thanks for asking,' and he smiled.

Later, when the shops reopened, she helped him choose cosmetics and a few other feminine fripperies, then they went into a supermarket and bought groceries.

'Maxine!' Guy protested, as they emerged with an outsize plastic bag full of tins of this and that. 'I'm not a blessed donkey! Your handbag,' he remembered. 'Come on, I know where we'll get a good one.'

Italy is famous for many things and not least for its leather goods. The handbags smelled of the tanning yard still, and were soft and pliable, some beautifully embossed, and all were very expensive.

'Still, if you want a good thing you have to pay for it,' said Guy Massey. 'Better than buying plastic rubbish.'

'You do understand I've got to pay you back?' demanded Margot.

'If you'd feel better.'

'Well, of course I would. And I want to pay my share of that wonderful meal.'

'You're not the daughter of Croesus, by any chance?'

'No, but I can pay my way. I think this cream one here. It's simple, tasteful, and hasn't got a long strap for a lout to grab hold of. I shan't keep money in it, anyhow. I won't be caught making the same mistake twice.'

'I wonder how often that remark has been made!' was Guy Massey's thoughtful rejoinder.

They were both quiet on the return journey to the village of Astria, and the car pulled in at the Villa Fiorita.

'No, don't bother getting out,' Guy Massey said, 'I'll dump my shopping and run you down to your place.'

'No need to bother,' said Margot. 'You've already done quite enough and it won't do me any harm to stretch my legs.'

'Why, hello!' It was the velvety voice of the woman Maxine. Her hair was obviously artificially bleached and her eyes a dancing blue. She was looking Margot up and down as she advanced from the small front porch. 'Whatever games have you two been up to, then?'

Guy made a playful pass at her chin. 'Cops and robbers, actually,' he said. 'Nurse Walsh was the victim of a bag snatcher.'

'Oh, you poor dear!' the other said promptly. 'Everywhere is gradually becoming like Chicago. Can I lend you some tights?'

'No, thanks,' replied Margot, 'I'll go home and have

a shower and change. Thank you very much, Doctor Massey, Mrs Massey.'

The woman laughed in sheer amusement as Guy went within.

'I'm not Mrs Massey,' she explained. 'My name's Derwent, Maxine Derwent. *Mrs* Maxine Derwent.'

'Oh, I'm sorry. I—well, goodbye.' Margot fled, her face scarlet, feeling a complete fool. What business was it of hers who was living with whom? One had to be broadminded these days. But Guy could have told her, spared her the embarrassment. But why should he? What was he to her that he owed her any explanations?

She rang the bell at the Villa Romana and Salvatore hobbled from his quarters to admit her. She could see that he was looking at her torn hose and making some comment, but she merely smiled and made her way to her own room. She could hear George squabbling with his little brother, accusing him of cheating in the game of chess they were playing. Young Van was a very good player and no doubt any moment George would dash the pieces and board to the floor in his fury at being beaten once more by a twelve-year-old.

Emily Whitham's voice was raised in complaint and then Margot shut them all out as she stripped and stepped into the shower. She didn't know whether she was glad to be back or not. She kept remembering her escort of the day, Guy Massey, almost against her will. First of all she saw him with the razor in his hand, regarding her, and then in the various faded blues of his clothes. Also she remembered the sharpness of her exchanges with him in the car. Actually she had been the one to come out fighting every time, when she recollected events, so that he had merely had to make an observation for her to take it as a personal insult. She remembered, and this was almost painful now, how glad she had been to see him in the museum, and how she had fallen into his arms like a lover and never wanted to leave them.

'I was emotional,' she decided as she towelled herself down. 'At least I knew him. I was looking for a familiar face and his was it. I'm sure he thought nothing of it. And anyway, he seems to be comfortably set up with Mrs Derwent and of no real interest to me. I don't suppose I shall ever forget Mike.'

She tried to recall Mike, but it was Guy Massey's mocking blue eyes which laughed back at her.

When she rejoined the Whitham family Mrs Whitham wanted to know how she had spent her day and was horrified by the handbag incident. George was uncommunicative, and when Margot addressed him he turned his head away deliberately. When she at length asked if there was anything she could do for him, he deigned to reply.

'It's still your day off, isn't it?' he demanded. 'Why don't you go out to a night-club to finish it off?'

'I might have,' she replied, 'if there were such things in Astria. But I think most of the population are in bed by nine o'clock. I can give you a talcum rub before dinner if you like?'

'No, thanks,' George said heavily, wheeling himself away. 'It's been quite a relief to have you out of my hair for once. I quite enjoyed your absence, actually.'

At this Parthian shaft Margot looked at his mother, who lowered her eyes.

'He's been a fiend,' she explained, 'and hasn't allowed any one of us to do a single thing for him. I really think he missed you, no matter what he says.'

'Oh, well, I won't leave him again if——'

'Rubbish!' returned Mrs Whitham. 'Doctor Massey thought you weren't getting out enough. You're George's nurse, you know, not his slave. I'm sorry your first day away from the villa was such a catastrophe. We used to stay in Rome, and there handbag snatching was rife. They even used to do it from cars. I didn't realise the practice had spread to Siena. Ah, I think I hear John arriving. I'll go and prepare his drink. I hope Giovanna has some ice; I told her to defrost the ice box.'

By morning George allowed Margot to attend to him, but he was not in a conversational mood. After she had helped him dress he said, 'I think I'll go back to bed. I feel tired today.'

'Oh! Well, have your swim and then go to bed. At least you'll have had some exercise.'

'I don't want to swim. I want to go back to bed.'

'Right!' Margot said without further argument. 'Back to pyjamas.'

'No, I'll just lie as I am under the counterpane. It's not a crime to feel tired, is it?'

'Not at all. I'd sometimes like to stay in bed all day and be waited on. Ecstasy!'

'That's because you can use your goddamned legs to get about!' he snapped. 'What difference is it to me whether I sit in a chair all day or lie in bed?'

'You're active from the waist up when you want to be,' replied Margot. 'A blind person develops other senses more acutely; someone in your position has to decide how to compensate for himself.'

'Big deal! All I ever get from you is platitudes and encouragement.'

'What *do* you want? Should I say "Poor George. What a shame!" all day long? Would *that* help?'

'No. Now you've washed me and fed me and powdered me in all the right places, like the great baby I am, please leave me to have my bye-byes in peace.'

Margot turned away almost angrily. She stopped in the doorway and counted to ten. 'No,' she told herself, 'don't let him rattle you or we're all sunk. This is something to do with leaving him yesterday. He's trying to make you pay for it today.'

It was a couple of hours before she returned to see how he was faring, and something made her creep the last few yards so that she could see through the fronds of a potted palm without being seen. George was sitting up in bed and gazing towards a bookcase on the other side of the room. As Margot watched he reached out towards his collapsible chair, but it was beyond his reach and he muttered in exasperation.

Margot was about to offer her help when she was stayed by the fact that George swung his useless legs over the edge of the bed and then slid out of sight. Her heart was thudding so that she fancied he might hear it, as he dragged himself on his strong arms backwards towards the bookcase. He selected a couple of books, threw them on to the bed and dragged himself back again. With a tremendous effort, which made him almost blue in the face, he pulled himself back on to the bed, straightened out his limbs neatly and pulled the quilt over them. He opened one of the books and began to read, still panting from his exertions.

Margot made a great to-do about approaching the second time when she brought George his milk and biscuits.

He pretended to open sleepy eyes and there was no sign of any books.

'My, what a lazybones you are!' she said cheerfully, automatically doing this and that and setting his chair in reach, just in case he wanted to make another excursion. 'Are you still happy to be left alone?'

'Yes, I'm O.K. You take another day off.'

'I won't do that, but I'll leave you till lunchtime.'

When she did bring his lunch he was genuinely fast asleep and the book he had been reading had slid from his fingers. Margot glanced at it. It was a textbook on law, and there were slivers of paper between the leaves with freshly written notes on them. As Margot held the book and looked down, George's eyes flickered open.

'What are you doing with that?' he suddenly demanded. 'It's mine.'

'I was just picking it up off the floor. Giovanna made you *canneloni*. She says it's nice and light.' She set the tray down on the bed-table, which swung across in front of him. '*Bon appétit*,' she wished.

'Did you see what I was reading?' he asked.

'I—er—think it was a law book. I'm not sure.'

'Well, listen! You're not to tell anybody else, see? I'm not going to law school like this and that's for sure. It's just that I was curious to see what we'd been doing— me and the other fellows—before my accident.'

'I see.'

'They'll all be miles ahead of me now.'

'But then you have a great deal of time on your hands, haven't you?'

'She's at it again! What a girl!' but a slow smile broke out on George's face and he was quite good-looking when he smiled. Margot smiled back at him. 'No telling anyone, eh?' he reminded her. 'When I'm good and ready I might—just might—get back to my studies. I'm not promising anything, though.'

CHAPTER FOUR

WHEN Margot arrived at Miss MacDougal's residence, she thought she was back in England—or maybe Scotland. The villa was so obviously British in character. It even had a roof of grey slate. Now where would one procure the materials for such a roof in Italy? The garden was British, too, a mass of rioting roses and delphiniums with hollyhocks stalking the boundary wall. A neat red-tiled porch, with seats either side, gave on to a blue-painted front door. Margot rang the bell and a dark-eyed girl of about sixteen answered.

'Who is that, Sophie?' a distant voice asked.

'Margot Walsh,' the newcomer confided, as obviously the maid spoke English. 'Please tell your mistress I've arrived for my lesson. I may be five minutes early.'

'Oh, she's not my mistress, she's my godmother. I'm here for the summer. My name's Sophia Lindsay. How do you do?'

Margot offered her hand. 'I'm awfully sorry.'

The girl smiled. 'That's all right. I'm always being taken for an Italian, but that's the Celt in me. I'm here to stay with Aunt Agnes for a while.'

Margot smiled and just then a room door opened and out stepped a blond-haired youth with soft, surprisingly dark, eyes which fastened upon Margot with interest. Behind him was a short, thin, ginger-haired old lady.

'All right, Riccardo, do your homework now. See him out, Sophia. Miss Walsh——?'

Miss MacDougal was no gossip. She gave instruction to English-speaking residents in Italian and to Italians in English. She said not one word to Margot outside the context of the lesson. Margot would have liked to know what a Scotswoman was doing resident here at all, but her mentor chivvied her along in the rudiments of Italian grammar and finally asked her goddaughter to show her out just as someone else was arriving.

Margot paused outside the garden gate to pack up her newly-acquired books, and was surprised when the previous student confronted her.

'Hello! I am Ricci Lamati. How do you do?'

Margot held out her hand almost instinctively and then wondered if she was being picked up.

'Have you been waiting here for an hour, Mr Lamati?'

'Oh, no. I locked up and came back. That is correct past tense, is it not? I thought perhaps I would like to see you home.'

'But why?'

'Because it is only good manners, I think. It is getting dark and you are attractive young lady. You should not walk alone.'

'Do you know where I live, Mr Lamati?'

'No, but you will tell me, please?'

Margot saw the red car coming and held up her hand to stop it.

'Thank you, Mr Lamati, but I'm being taken home.'

'Ah, good!' he opened the door of the Alfa Romeo and she slid inside, not meeting Guy Massey's questioning gaze. 'Perhaps I see you again soon? I like to practise my English.'

'A new boy-friend?' asked Guy Massey as the car roared forward.

'Hardly,' Margot responded. 'He's a fellow student at Miss MacDougal's.'

'I've seen him hanging about the village. I don't think he's a local. I'm glad I came along; I thought next Thursday we might visit the caves along the coast. Maxine will make us a picnic.'

'Is she coming too?'

'No. She would say that three's a crowd.'

'Then why don't you just take her?'

'Because she sees enough of me. It's nice to get away from each other once in a while.'

Margot was silent as they approached the Villa Romana, and then she got out as he opened the passenger door and confronted him in the twilight.

'Look, Doctor Massey, I don't know what your relationship with Mrs Derwent is—I don't want to know— but I do know that in her shoes I would resent preparing a picnic for you to share with somebody else. I would rather have no part in it, thank you.'

'My relationship with Maxine?' he laughed disbelievingly. 'I can tell you what that is. She's my sister. My *twin* sister.'

'Then why didn't she tell me, when I addressed her as Mrs Massey?'

'Didn't she? Probably because it amused her to have you thinking the worst, which you did. *Honi soit qui mal y pense*, Nurse Walsh.'

'I'm sorry. Gosh, but I seem to put my foot in things with you, Doctor Massey. But you *are* married? *Were* married? Oh lord, don't say I've done it again!'

'I was married for two months when I was twenty-two, and still a student, against all advice,' he said gravely. 'I married a girl under sentence of death from leukaemia. The depth of my pity was more than akin to love. It *was* love, concentrated because of the time limit. I could not have loved so well had it been longer drawn out. No, don't say you're sorry yet again. It's all a long time ago and one does forget. Now, *are* you coming next Thursday, or not?'

Margot said, ashamed, 'If I won't be in the way, and you're sure you wouldn't rather be doing something else, yes, I would like to.'

'Good! You're so self-effacing, Nurse Walsh, that I can't believe you're true at times. When you're not being self-effacing you're spitting like a wildcat. I'll be in to see our friend some time during the weekend. How is he?'

'I caught him reading his law books today and taking notes. It was all done by stealth and I have not to tell anyone. I suppose it doesn't count telling you.'

'Good for George! He just might come to grips with his fate before he succeeds in driving his family mad. Keep up the good work.'

When Margot had her second Italian lesson, once more

the fair-haired, dark-eyed Italian youth was waiting for her, obviously not feeling the least snubbed or put out by her behaviour on the previous occasion, and this time the red car did not come along to rescue her.

He fell into step beside her, offering to carry her books.

'You live at the Villa Romana, yes? The big house.'

'How do you know?'

'Because I asked around. I have a room in the village just for the summer. I am a medical student at university in Rome, actually, but I have a vacation job. You understand my English, yes? Good! Miss MacDougal say all Italian put 'a' on the end of words and to be most careful not to.'

'What is your job?' Margot asked, trying to appear interested.

'I am caretaker of the Terracini castle and church,' Ricci told her. 'I take people round and earn a little money. I must also pick up litter and keep things tidy—not much of a job, but better than nothing. Also I get chance to speak English with tourists. Mostly they are American or English. They come on excursion which includes a visit to the ruins and the church.'

'How interesting!'

'Have you seen the ruins and the church?'

'No. I——'

'Well, for you no charge. Private viewing. You be my guest.'

'I don't get much time off duty,' said Margot. 'I'm a nurse, you see. The eldest son of the people in the villa is a paraplegic.'

Ricci sobered. 'Oh! You mean he cannot walk? That

is terrible. I would like to meet him, cheer him up, you know?'

'I don't think he's ready to be cheered up just yet, Mr Lamati, and I can't invite people to the villa. I'm just an employee.'

'Oh, yes, I see. My name is Ricci, you know, from Riccardo. Mr Lamati is too formal, I think, if we are going to be friends?'

'Well, Ricci, I don't know about that. I——'

'Your name, please?' Ricci was so unabashed she felt ashamed.

'Margot. Margot Walsh.'

'That is a very easy English name to remember. We have an English Student at university called Sisselswaite. I can't say it. I try, but I can't.'

She laughed. 'You mean Thistlethwaite? I'm not surprised. Well, Ricci, here's the villa and I must go.'

'Then when I see you again?'

She couldn't withstand the gaze of those imploring brown eyes. She didn't want to encourage him, but had not the heart to discourage him.

'I have these two hours free every day, from five until seven. Perhaps I could visit the ruins tomorrow?'

He went away, rather dashing in his lightweight cream suit, with the patterned shirt that was open almost to his navel. She wondered if he came from the north, for many northern Italians were both blond and blue-eyed. His hair was beautiful, wavy and ending in tiny curls. Many a girl would have envied the boy his hair.

All thoughts of Mr Riccardo Lamati left her as the reality of George impinged. George was not at all beautiful with his short sandy hair and sharp blue eyes, as well as his uncertain temper. Apparently Mr Whitham was home, for they were having a row, he and his son, and Margot slid away so that she could not overhear. She came upon Emily, who looked distraught.

'Now John's ulcer will play up and he won't want to eat. The trouble is he'll still have his ration of drink. He's hitting the bottle more and more. Oh, God, why did it have to happen to us?'

Margot was still regarding her as she looked up and she said apologetically, 'I know. Everybody must ask the same question at times. Why is my child blind, or sub-normal, or a deaf-mute, or injured in an accident so he'll never walk again? We'll never know the answers.'

'Perhaps tackling the problem is the only real answer,' said Margot.

'Is that a criticism of me and my family, Nurse?'

'Oh, no. I'm sorry if that's what it sounded like. I—I think there's an improvement in George, but I can't really say more. Please don't ask me. If you could persuade your husband not to force issues you may be pleasantly surprised one of these days.'

'You hold out a ray of hope and say I mustn't question you?' asked Mrs Whitham.

'That's right. I'm a little more in George's confidence than I was. I think he finds it easier to confide in a stranger. If I lose his confidence now, then we might be back to square one. Please keep your patience, both with him and me.'

A glowering Mr Whitham passed her as she went in to George, who greeted her appearance by hurling a tumbler to the floor where it shattered into a hundred slivers.

'I hope that made you feel better,' she said calmly.

'Would you like me to fetch another?'

'He's been on to me,' George raged, 'about some idiot son of a fellow in Turin who's been chosen for the Paraplegic World Games as a discus thrower. All is not lost, you know, if you can throw the wretched discus further than the other chairbound competitors. What an ambition!'

'Any ambition would be an improvement,' Margot said as she swept up the pieces of glass, 'except that of demoralising and destroying your family. That one's going very well.'

'What do you mean?' George asked.

'Would it make your day to know the truth?' she jeered. 'I'm not going to encourage you. I'm not going to give you the satisfaction of knowing how well you're doing.'

'No, no kidding,' George said seriously. 'What did you mean about destroying my family?'

'You *must* have noticed how changed things are these past two years?' asked Margot. 'Your father with an ulcer and aiming to become an alcoholic, your mother in a state of nervous depression. Even I have noticed a change since I joined you. This past week you've won more chess games against Van than ever before. Right? Well, that's not because you've improved, it's because he doesn't want to upset you by beating you all the time.'

'You're lying!' George flared. 'You're lying in your teeth!'

'Oh no, I'm not. And Tessa's planning never to marry. She's going to devote her life to looking after you. She told me so herself, poor kid! And your mother and father feel guilty ... your father for leaving that wretched car with the keys in it and your mother for not being able to drive, because then she'd have had her own car which you could have borrowed. The whole family goes round and round in circles. If only—if only——'

'It's not true,' George said, 'you're making it all up.'

'Oh no, I'm not, George. You've wrapped yourself up in your own troubles and haven't given anyone else a thought. You're the most selfish person I ever met.'

George bit his lip and turned his face away.

'Please go,' he said, and Margot was so startled at his use of the word 'please' that she stared at him. 'Please go and leave me. I'll have supper on a tray. You've made me very unhappy, if that's what you intended.'

'No, that's not what I intended. I simply thought you ought to know that other people are bearing your burden unnecessarily heavily. Somebody's going to crack soon, unless there's hope of improvement in this family's relations.'

'I thought I asked you to go.'

'Yes—sorry. I'm going. I'll have your supper sent to you.'

Margot felt upset herself all evening, wondering if she had gone too far. Giovanna must have been upset that her culinary efforts went practically untasted. Now Margot noticed how much John Whitham drank and how little he ate, how Emily picked at her food and looked at him and away again, how Tessa made patterns on her salad with dressing but seemed hardly to be there, and how young Van, who was always hungry, only had two helpings of ice-cream while the rest took coffee. There was practically no conversation during the meal. It was as though George's absence from the table inhibited everybody more than when he was there. His disquieting spirit brooded everywhere. Margot was glad when she could make her excuses and leave the dining room to go to him.

He was sitting in his chair gazing out over the dark garden. On the road in the distance, without accompanying sound, the headlamps of cars occasionally appeared and flashed before they disappeared round a bend.

'Well, George, do you feel like going to bed?' she asked.

'Bed!' he rounded on her. 'I'd like to go to bed and never get up again! It's all just too damned difficult!'

She hesitated to approach him, then he spoke again.

'I'm sorry! I'd practically decided to turn over a new leaf, and there it goes, with a blot on it.'

'Never mind,' said Margot, 'there's always another.'

'I've been thinking about what you said, about Mother feeling that some of the guilt was hers, simply because she couldn't drive and so never owned a car. We used to tease her about it a lot. All the other kids used to be picked up from school by their mothers, but we had to depend on other people or take a bus. We never minded, only teased her. We used to tease each other a lot; have fun.'

'I can imagine,' Margot said softly.

'And Dad always liked his drink, with ice, in the evenings. Only one, and accompanied by a nice fat Havana cigar. I can remember being allowed to light it for him and thinking there was no smell in the world like it, and no dad like him. I only ever wanted my dad to be proud of me. I'd have done anything to please him.'

'Why don't you still want——?'

'Look,' he exclaimed, 'shut up, will you? There goes page number two. Tear it out! How come Mother didn't tell me about her feelings of guilt? And why does Dad always try to make me be like some other cripple in a wheelchair? Why do you know so much about my family that I don't know?'

'Perhaps it's the old one about the observer seeing most of the game. But if in any way I can be the catalyst that gets you back to being a happy family again, then I'll be content. I caught you reading your law books the other day, George. Now why don't you let me tell your father that? It would make him very happy.'

'Because I'm not sure yet if that's what I want to do. I have to think and decide, and you've got to help me. I know now that I can't make them suffer any longer. I'll go into a sanatorium, if they like. How does that strike you?'

'As the line of least resistance. Yes, I suppose you could go into some sort of private hospital at home, and be with others of your kind, and get out of your family's hair at least. But taking on the world on the outside, with a handicap, would be the real challenge. Perhaps your family needs you to be whole again. Tell me how I can help you?'

'I want you to get me a few books, and lots of writing materials,' George said eagerly. 'I still have the test paper for the law exam I never took. When I feel I can tackle it confidently, then I'll tell Dad, and he'll no doubt arrange for me to have a tutor. I don't want to build up his hopes and then let him down again. I'll try to be—you know—more tolerant with the family. I can't promise anything, but you held a mirror up to me earlier, Nurse dear, and I sure didn't like what I saw.'

That evening seemed to be the nadir that preceded the slow rising of the sun again in the Whitham family's life. All next day Margot watched her patient anxiously, feeling that the sarcastic rejoinder must come when his mother asked him, as usual, how he was.

'Fine, thank you,' he replied, however, and Mrs Whitham started visibly.

'You're sure?'

'Of course I'm sure. Hey, isn't Tessa looking good today?' Tessa was drying herself after her swim. Her graceful long-legged figure was outlined against the shimmering blue of the pool. 'Say, Tess, you got any boyfriends yet? Tell them they've got to answer to me first, will you?'

Emily looked questioningly at Margot, who put a finger meaningfully to her lips.

They had lunch together on the terrace, and still George kept up the good work. Margot felt proud of him.

'Do you want a game of chess after siesta, George?' asked young Van, dubiously.

'Yes, if you've nothing else on. But only on condition that you go ahead and beat me if you can, or else tell me what I'm about to do wrong, so that I get as good as you are eventually, huh? Don't think I haven't noticed how you've been playing rotten games lately, so that I won. I don't want you to let me off leniently. So long as that's understood?'

Van beamed. 'Yes, George. I'll teach you the Sicilian gambit. We'll have a good game.'

When the time came for Margot to take her two hours off duty, she was almost sorry she had made arrangements to go out. Surely George might lapse in her absence. She asked him if he would prefer her to stay home.

'Why should I?' he asked. 'You go. Have a good time.'

'I'm only going to have a look at the old estate,' she told him. 'I could do that any time. It'll still be there.'

'Then you go and do just that. Tell me all about it later.'

'And if your father's home before I get back——?'

'Don't worry, Nurse. I'll be a good boy, I promise.'

Margot went off into the open air trying to relax as after a hard day's work. Actually her work had not been hard that day, it was the tension of watching George behave himself which had tied her up into knots. She was so lost in thought that she almost bumped into Guy Massey on the road. He was accompanied by a large, hairy dog which leapt up at Margot, gave her a fond lick and, being heavier than she was, bowled her over backwards into the roadside grass.

'There!' Guy's blue eyes were laughing as he helped her up and brushed her down. He paused with his hands on her slim waist and said, 'She likes you.'

Margot removed his hands pointedly. 'What a relief!' she said. 'I should hate to think what would have happened to me had she not. What is it, anyway?'

'Sh, don't offend her by calling her an *it*. Teresa is a cross between a St Bernard and a Pryrenean mountain dog. She's supposed to be good with sheep and excellent in the snow. I can guarantee she can scatter a flock of sheep or goats further than anybody, and her experience in snow is somewhat limited in Astria. She's Doctor

Agostini's dog and we're going walkies to deliver a pre-
scription. Eh, Teresa?'

'Woof!' agreed the monster in a deep *basso profundo*,
and made a skittering turn in the dust of the road,
wagging a great fan of a tail.

'You taking a walk too?' asked Guy Massey.

'No, I'm going to see the ruins,' she responded.

'Oh. Well, they're worth seeing. Until Thursday, then?'

Margot continued on her way, the thought of her next
meeting with Guy Massey a pleasing picture.

CHAPTER FIVE

MARGOT found the door in the wall open and heard
young voices raised in laughter. She saw Ricci Lamati
and with him was Miss MacDougal's pretty Sophia. There
was an area of rich grassland, velvet-soft, and an archery
target set up. Ricci was showing Sophia how to hold a
bow and his arms were around her. They were both
giggling and it all looked very innocent. Margot smiled
indulgently as she said, 'Hello!'

Ricci looked round. 'Oh, Margot—hello! You were
late. I am trying to show Sophia how to shoot arrows, but
she is a very bad pupil.'

'Can you do it, Ricci?' asked Margot.

'Oh, yes. When I am alone here I have to do something, and I am now getting quite good. I show you?'

He went back some distance and took an arrow from
a sling. As he drew back the bowstring, with his slight,
graceful figure and blond curling hair, she was reminded

of a classical statue. He could have been Cupid at that moment, fluid and beautiful. The arrow pinged just left of the bullseye, and he laughed.

'Jolly good!' Margot applauded. 'I like your sports arena, too. Do you have to cut the grass?'

'One of my more menial tasks, but now it shouldn't need doing again until autumn, and I will be gone by then.'

'I really ought to get back to godmother,' Sophia said regretfully.

'O.K.' agreed Ricci. 'You come for another lesson to-morrow, eh?' He was folding up the heavy target and Margot followed him as he dragged it into a sort of vestry off the small church nearby and locked the door.

'Come and see!' he invited, reaching out to take her hand in his and leading her into the church by the main doors. 'Now isn't that beautiful?'

Margot gazed round the little church in absolute amazement. It was tiny, with wonderfully carved oak bench seats for no more than a dozen, possibly the maximum capacity of the ancient Terracini family. The walls were painted blue and the whole place gave the impression of a grotto, with the light coming from a glass dome in the roof. Flutings between the glass panels were exquisitely painted with flying cherubim, sashes from their trumpets entwining their tiny bodies and floating behind them, again in an exquisite shade of blue.

'It's wonderful!' Margot said, almost reverently. 'What a pity people can't worship here any more!'

'Oh, some do,' Ricci said airily. 'They don't know any better. Look what I do to help them!'

He slipped into a small aperture behind the reredos and

brought out a wooden statue of the Blessed Virgin, which he set down, and then disappeared to bring a vulgar-looking picture displaying a large bleeding heart, which he propped up against the altar, and finally he appeared with a multiple candle-holder in which most of the candles were half burnt or more. A box of matches was obligingly supplied in its own slot.

'People light candles for loved ones, say prayers,' he explained. 'They pay money to light a candle. When they leave I blow out all the candles again.'

'But how can they do such things in a church which no longer has a licence for worship? It's like praying in a museum.'

He shrugged. 'Can I help it if people want to pray? I only put out the statue, the picture and the candles and it makes them feel good. People do not only say prayers in churches with licences. They pray at home. Prayer is in the heart.' He seemed to have sensed her disapproval. 'This is a very badly paid job I am doing. I am expected to take tips, and the candles are one of the perks—you say?'

'It's no business of mine, Ricci,' said Margot, and stood up. She would have liked to have visited the little church alone, and sat on one of the bench seats and tried to dream up the past, but the hint of commercialism now about the scene upset her. She turned to leave while Ricci bundled his various products away behind the reredos. She had an idea that they had never belonged to the Terracini family, that maybe Ricci—or his predecessor—had purchased them in some junk shop in the hope of persuading visitors to part with their money in an artificially induced emotional moment.

He joined her outside and took her hand like a child who wishes to be forgiven some misdemeanour.

'I will show you the rest of the castle, yes?'

The castle, what was left of it, had obviously been subject recently to the hands of the preservers. New cement joined old stones together and there were a couple of new flying buttresses propping up ancient walls. It stood on the edge of a rocky cliff and, no doubt, in winter was exposed to violent elements.

Ricci gave her a guided tour of the various rooms, though all the roof had crumbled and the stones and ancient tiles were piled up neatly in corners, with tough grass growing between and round the heaps. Below thundered the sea, eternally battering the rocky headland.

'Can you keep a big secret?' Ricci asked with an impish smile.

'I don't know. If you've found the Terracini treasure I would have to tell someone,' and Margot laughed to take any sting out of her words.

'Oh, no treasure, worse luck, or I wouldn't even tell you. This is something else—an adventure. But I haven't told anybody else about it.'

'I'm honoured.'

'Come with me. Don't be frightened, I will look after you.'

Margot hadn't realised how windy it would be on the exposed promontory with the west wall of the castle behind them and nothing now between them and the breaking white swirl of waves on the rocks below but a narrow plateau on which only the toughest grass grew. Ricci, his golden hair flying in the wind, was standing on the very edge and pointing over.

'You follow me down,' he said. 'It's only a little way and I will watch you don't fall. You are not afraid?' he challenged.

'I don't think so.' But as she peered over the edge she felt faint at the sight of that boiling sea and the black basalt rocks which were exposed at intervals.

Ricci had disappeared over the edge, and she now saw he was standing on a ledge which couldn't have been more than eighteen inches wide.

'Come on!' he shouted against the wind and the thunder of the waves. Kneeling down, she poked with an investigating foot and found it grasped by Ricci. 'Come on! You're O.K.!' he encouraged, and she slid over the edge to find herself, heart pounding, on the ledge beside her friend.

'Now for the adventure!' he told her, his merry eyes regarding her speculatively. 'You look very fright, Margot,' he told her.

'I am—very fright,' she acknowledged. 'Frightened,' she remembered to correct him.

'Don't be—frightened. The worst is over. Look!'

He lifted up a tangle of tough hanging grass and sea-pinks and exposed a hole in the cliff face. He disappeared on hands and knees through it and called her to follow. She knew she had laddered yet another pair of tights as she did so, but now the small opening became deeper and she could stand up. Ricci had produced a torch and was guiding the way. The thunder of the sea was magnified as though the tunnel acted as a megaphone, and it was as though one was in the midst of it and drowning. Margot felt the panic of claustrophobia and gasped for breath and then Ricci caught hold of her arm and said, 'You see?'

They were standing in a large cave which was like a subterranean room. The floor was flat and at intervals rocks stuck out like tables and chairs. The roof was eight or nine feet high and Margot's panic stilled, for all was dry in here. There was dusty soil on the floor and a pallid cluster of fungi grew in a corner.

'I found this one day when I was collecting seagull eggs,' Ricci explained. 'We are underneath the castle. I have studied old maps and I think there should be a way up into the castle, but I haven't found it yet. I think this was a place for hiding in olden times of wars when Italy was many countries. Don't you find it very interesting?'

'Very,' said Margot, moving around and looking at this and that avidly. She had a strange feeling that if she stayed still and faced Ricci something would happen, and it was something she would regret. She didn't know why she didn't like Ricci, who was so beautiful and so charming. Twice or thrice he had retreated when she had appeared to object to their physical contact of hand- or arm-holding, but here, in this underground cavern, she was so absolutely at his mercy if he felt disposed to take advantage of her. She told herself that he was only a boy, George's age, but still she almost jumped as she felt his hands resting on her shoulders.

'Look up!' he said, this time not moving his hands even when she shrugged most obviously. 'You see those marks on the roof?'

'A sort of square,' she said, and added, 'I really must be going. They'll be wondering where I've got to at the villa.'

'I have a theory about what you see up there,' said Ricci, ignoring the second part of her statement. 'I think there is the way into this place from the castle above. If I can find that stone slab on the surface I'm sure, with a —with a—what is that large piece of iron which lifts things?'

'A crowbar?'

'That is right. With a crowbar I will uncover the mystery.' His right hand, so lightly, contoured her shoulder and breast and stayed on her waist for a moment during which his dark eyes stared almost hypnotically into hers and then, when he gained no response, laughed again. 'But you want to go. I am too terrible for keeping you here like this. Come!'

He led the way to the exit and that terrifying scramble up the cliff face, where she really needed his help and so clung to him, quivering with relief, when they were on terra firma again. But his touch—it may have been the Latin in him—had created in her a feeling of revulsion. Once at the cliff top she begun to run, eager to get away, wondering if Ricci would follow her and then she found her outlet in other arms and subsided against a width of masculine chest.

'I'll take you home, Margot,' said Guy Massey. To Ricci he said, 'The side gate was open. You don't want gipsies to get in here, do you?'

'No, sir. No. I will lock up now. Goodnight, Margot. I see you, I expect.'

'Goodnight.'

Arms about each other, Guy and Margot walked towards the Villa Romana. They did not speak, but she leant her head against his shoulder, feeling suddenly and deliciously tired as after physical exercise.

Outside the villa, with now only a faint phosphorescent glow from the evening sky, before he rang the bell which would summon Salvatore, Guy suddenly held her away from him and said, 'I fancied earlier that you came running to me for help, but I must warn you that with women I take what I want.'

She was seized so strongly and so brutally that not even a whimper of protest could escape her as his mouth pressed down firmly upon hers. She felt dazed, then outraged, then elated and enhanced as a woman. Then his fierce hold relaxed and his hands slid down so that they merely touched her own fingertips.

'Well?' Margot found herself asking the more sharply that she was covering her inner confusion. 'Have you taken what you want? Is that all?'

'For the present,' he decided, and added nastily, 'your evening has no doubt been busy enough already.' He made to ring the bell and hesitated. 'What were you running from?' he asked. 'What had he done to you, that young Romeo? Why were you looking as though you'd been dragged through a hedge backwards?'

Little thrills were running through her body down to her toes, so that she felt weak and rather wonderful. He was asking the questions as though he really minded and would prefer not to know the answers he feared, but silence would be akin to a lie. Whatever was to be between them, there must be no lies.

'Actually I don't know why I was running,' she said, 'and Ricci hadn't done anything to me, only shown me round the castle. I—I certainly haven't been dragged through a hedge backwards, in the way I think you mean.

We'd been scrambling around a bit, exploring.' She didn't mention the cave. That was Ricci's secret and he had asked her not to tell anyone.

'Well, I'm sorry.' It was obvious to her that Guy sounded relieved and not a bit sorry. 'I rather barged in, in that case. I don't know much about young Lamati, but I feel you ought to know that young Italians do enjoy having temporary affairs with visiting young women. They have a natural charm and live on their emotions. They die of heartbreak very easily and recover spontaneously. I must sound like a dutch uncle.'

'I certainly preferred you in your earlier rôle,' teased Margot.

It was too dark for her now to see him, but a short laugh came out of the darkness.

'Yes, I think I preferred it, too.' The bell rang at last. The powerful lights on either side of the gateway came on and then they heard Salvatore's shuffle over the gravelled walk.

'Are you—really—a danger to me?' she asked softly.

He reached out, took her right hand and raised her fingertips to his lips.

'I'll tell you—on Thursday,' he promised, and was gone as Salvatore closed the gate after her. He was saying something about the family being already at dinner and Margot had to collect herself, realising that the Withams would have waited and waited for her to come before they actually began the meal. She owed them some sort of explanation. She entered the dining-room, and Mr Witham stood up.

'No, please, do carry on,' she said more calmly than she could have believed. 'I'll get myself a tray later. I must shower—I'm in rather a mess. I got knocked over by a dog—Doctor Agostini's dog. It's huge. Have you seen it? *Bon appétit.*'

She fled, and it was only as she stood under the shower that she realised, wrapped up in her own private thoughts as she had been, that what she had disturbed was a scene of harmony and family togetherness. There had been quiet chat as she had entered the room, and one of the voices had been George's, talking to his father. Now she saw the scene again, and everybody had been relaxed, John Whitham's glass half-raised to his lips, which he had set down upon the table to stand up on her arrival.

'George must still be keeping it up,' she decided, for George's earlier behaviour and his insistence that she must go out seemed way back in the past rather than merely a few hours ago. Somehow she had managed to live a small lifetime since she ran into those widely stretched arms Guy had held to receive her, and all that had happened subsequently. She acknowledged a newly realised truth to herself. Years did not make up living, it was moments: it was the gold shining through the dross, the oyster which nourished the pearl beyond price, that contact with the lips of a man who warned her off him yet had kissed like a lover. Wasn't it her mother who had said, 'Happiness comes in small doses,' when she had been at her happiest with Mike? And Aunt Kate, her mother's older, spinster sister who had chilled the moment with her typical response, 'And so does poison, and don't you ever forget it.'

Some kind of reaction set in so that Margot's personal excitement and happiness dissipated quickly into a kind of depression. Fortunately George, when he came to bed, was tired and not inclined to hold conversation. He simply said, 'I'm exhausted with being a good boy, so just do what you must, Nurse, and let me sleep.'

So she was at last alone in her own room, with her thoughts and recollections. Of course she had cheapened herself by throwing herself into Guy Massey's arms. If he thought she was frightened of Ricci, which he obviously had done by his later remarks, then it had been merely acting on her part, a means to an end which had been of her deliberate contriving, because now she had to acknowledge to herself that she *was* attracted to Guy Massey, and had been since that first time she had known the comfort of his arms in the museum in Siena.

His threat of taking 'what he wanted' from women had not killed off this attraction but stimulated it. It had made her feel raw and vulnerable and primitively anxious to please. Why, what must he be thinking of her to apparently welcome his attentions after his initial announcement! She should have pounded his chest with balled fists during that assault, so that he would know she was not that sort of girl, but nothing could smother the remembrance of the primeval delight of the act of kissing a man who made it feel like the discovery of all adult experience. Why (compared to those for him) her feelings for Mike were those of a child for its favourite uncle.

Still, she determined that Guy Massey would not get another chance like that. If he thought that on Thursday they would continue where they had left off, then he was mistaken. She had discovered the wanton in her own nature in good time, fortunately, and so far nobody was hurt.

In her dreams she ran round and round in an underground maze, growing ever more panic-stricken until she found Guy at the end of a tunnel, and, all unknowing of her conscious vow, proceeded to rush into his arms and demand his kisses.

George was more communicative in the morning and rather sober.

'I guess I've been so wrapped up in myself I've been blind to everything else,' he told Margot as she gave his legs a massage and covered him liberally in talc. 'I didn't know my dad had had a slight coronary last winter. My God, he might've died! Why didn't Mother tell me about it? "All's well that ends well", she said, but the very idea of feeling she couldn't confide a thing like that! I must've been a real pain in the neck.

'Anyway,' he continued, 'I was waiting for Dad when he came home, and I asked Mother to leave us alone. I poured Dad a drink, and I had one myself. We had a long talk. I told him I was ready to do whatever he thought was best for me and the family. I would go in a sanatorium and not moan about it, or I'd face the world and do a job commensurate with my disability, if he'd back me. My dad cried. I never thought I'd live to see the day ...'

'People don't only cry when they're miserable,' Margot said quickly. 'They cry when they're relieved and happy.'

'Yes, I know, because I cried, too, when Dad looked at me and said, "Well done, son! That's my boy!"' George swallowed. 'Anyway, I thought you'd like to know that I'm sort of committed to my law studies. I can't back out now. Dad's getting me a tutor. As I'll never qualify for sainthood I may occasionally take things out on you, Nurse. Will you mind?'

'Not at all, I'm tough,' she smiled. 'Fight me all you
want.'

'Where did you get to last night?'

'Oh!' She hid her momentary confusion in packing the
oil and talcum away. 'I was taken on a tour of the old
church and castle. It was all most interesting.'

'Who took you round? Is there a guide?'

'Yes. He's a young medical student—your age—very
charming. He wants to meet you. To cheer you up, he
said.'

George grinned. 'Poor devil! He must be short of
company.'

'I think he is. Astria isn't exactly Rome, and he gets
bored when he's not showing visitors round. He likes to
practise his English, which is why he seized on to Sophia
and me.'

'Who's Sophia?'

'Oh, she's the goddaughter of the language teacher,
Miss MacDougal. She's Scottish, but looks Italian. On
the other hand Ricci, who *is* Italian, is very blond.'

'Some of them dye their hair, you know,' he told her.

'Oh, George! Go on!'

'Yes, they do. I read somewhere that it's the "in" thing
to have blond hair with brown eyes. I'll bet this Ricci has
brown eyes?'

'Yes, he has, but——'

'Anyway, I'll see myself. He needn't come and cheer
me up, I'll go and look round his castle. Do you think I
could make it?'

'You can do anything you set your mind to, George.

I'll help, of course. I'll tell Ricci and arrange for you to have a private tour.'

George was not immediately an angel, by any means. During that day he almost lost his temper on several occasions, but always he managed to drag himself back from the brink of his tantrums and engage quickly in some activity. He was at his happiest when he could openly retire to his room and bring out his books for a couple of hours. Margot saw him as little as was absolutely necessary; she realised he must learn to do without her if he was really to take his place in the world eventually. It would have to be a slow withdrawal from dependence, and this summer might see it through. They would all have to wait and see.

Margot was still rehearsing as she ate her solitary breakfast on Thursday morning. It promised to be a blazing hot day and she was dressed coolly in white, with navy pipings round neck and hem. Her plan of action was ready. If Guy made any advance to her she would say, quietly, so as not to give offence, 'I don't think we should make a habit of this sort of thing, Doctor Massey. It's not as if we really know one another very well, is it?' Then he would respond with something like, 'I don't wish to offend you, Nurse Walsh, but I find you so attractive I can't keep my hands off you. You must forgive me. I'm only a man.'

It was then up to her to reassure him a little without encouraging his masculine ego too far. 'I don't see any reason why we shouldn't get to know one another better, Doctor. What's wrong with our being friends?' '*Platonic* friends?' he would reply, and she would then

cast her eyes down coyly and look at him again to say,
'Why not, at first? Friendships can develop in so many
ways.'

Salvatore came, out of breath, to announce that the
dottore was waiting at the gate and anxious to be off.

Margot forgot her cool collectedness, and half-scalded
herself drinking her second cup of coffee at one gulp. She
picked up a holdall containing her bathing things, donned
a pretty white leghorn straw hat she had bought locally,
and ran for the gate, which stood open.

Far from sweeping her into a mad embrace, Guy
Massey looked at her disapprovingly.

'Why are you dressed for a garden party?' he demanded. 'I thought I made it clear we're going rock-
scrambling?'

'How am I supposed to dress for that?' she asked, a
little sharply. 'I'm not a hippy with tattered old jeans
among my things.'

'Well, let's go. Better take off the hat, though. It will
blow away.'

The car shot off and took the high road which led
tourists away from the village of Astria. Not many
tourists had actually discovered Astria was there at all,
apart from those who came by coach to view the ruins
and then descend on the *trattoria* where they were re-
galed with a glass of Chianti and vanilla-flavoured or
almond pastries, included in the cost of the excursion.
Those who preferred coffee or the local beer paid extra
and dearly for the privilege.

Astria was a village of only about four hundred souls,
most of the male population were fishermen and their
sons and, nowadays, even their daughters left home as

soon as they could to work in the cities and live their own lives and raise families there. Astria only had a small, stony beach and was not pretty.

After about an hour, during which Guy Massey had merely pointed out places of passing interest, such as a boys' town community run by local monks, and the oldest olive tree in Tuscany, lovingly railed in and purported to have been there at the time of St Paul's journeys, they turned down a winding track and arrived in a cove which was an amphitheatre of black rocks and deep, dark pools.

'We seem to have the place to ourselves,' Margot remarked, climbing out of the car and deciding that here it was all going to begin again, with the sounding sea as a backcloth to her sweet reasoning. She trembled when Guy brushed against her as he reached into the car. She half closed her eyes as he straightened up again.

'Well?' he asked. 'Aren't you going to change into something else?' She looked at him fully in astonishment.

'What for?' she asked. He had peeled off his shirt, showing a disturbing width of masculine brown chest and now unselfconsciously unzipped his pants. She turned her back, her heart pounding.

'You've brought your swimming gear, haven't you? I *did* tell you.'

'Yes, I have,' she said breathlessly. 'Where can I change?'

He walked past her in blue swimming trunks.

'Anywhere you like. There's nobody about. I'll be round the bluff.'

Margot began to be a little annoyed with Guy. The night before last might never have been the way he was treating her today, disapproving of her dress and telling

her to do this and that, almost as though she was slightly
in the way rather than the companion of his choice.

She had never liked bikinis and wore a one-piece swimming costume in a shade of daffodil yellow. She went
round the bluff he had mentioned, wishing she had
brought espadrilles for her feet. The rocks were sharp,
each made up of thousands of tiny volcanic fragments.
Before her was a natural swimming pool, oval in shape,
and going to and fro with a powerful crawl stroke was
Guy Massey, who did not even pause to welcome her, or
so it seemed.

'You *do* swim?' he paused to ask; so he had noticed
her, she thought bitterly. 'Because it's thirty feet deep
here in parts.'

'I'll try to keep on top,' she said sarcastically, and took
the plunge. It was so cold she gasped in shocked surprise
and looked at her companion, who smiled wryly.

'It's fresh water, believe it or not,' he said, and pointed
to the nearby cliff where a stream gushed out of the face
about twenty metres up. 'That probably travels underground from the Alps. All is possible! Take your exercise
and then we'll warm up. I find this very therapeutic, and
so, I hope, will you.'

They lay on towels, baking in the unbelievable heat
thereafter, and still he hadn't said one tender word.

'Now we'll have a scramble up the cliffs,' he said. 'You
need something on your feet. I have a pair of brogues
that Maxine uses, in the car boot. How big are your
shoes?'

Margot raised one bare leg and stretched her toes in
an unconsciously sensuous movement, knowing her feet
were on the small side and perfect.

'You may have to stuff the toes. Maxine takes English sixes. I'll bring some newspaper.'

She did not feel particularly glamorous wearing somebody else's brogues with a swimming costume, but she followed her companion along the rocky coastline, climbing this rock and that, scrambling up the cliff to holes which were not really caves but looked it from ground level, and then down again to impede the progress of a crab, perhaps, and watch it trying to evade their reaching hands, and popping mermaids' purses, which Guy did far better than she with a satisfactory explosion each time, and then back to the natural swimming pool.

'Right!' said Guy, removing his sandals. 'A final swim for appetite and then we can get dressed and have our picnic.'

She had an odd desire to gain his attention, and felt that though they had now been together for four hours he hadn't really noticed her. She discarded the borrowed brogues and walked round the freshwater pool to seek a point of high vantage. Maybe a really good dive, if she could bring it off, would make him pay heed.

He was once again going to and fro, using his powerful stroke and leaving a white wake behind his feet. She was now poised to dive, uncomfortably aware that the water lay ten feet or so below, a much higher dive than she had ever attempted before. The moment before she launched herself she heard Guy's voice shout, 'No, you idiot! Not there! Flatten out——!'

Margot saw to her horror a ledge of rock approaching her under about two feet of water and literally flattened out, thus performing the most painful belly-flop of her career. She was winded and sore, and in no mood to be lifted out of the water like a half-drowned puppy and laid in the sun to be scolded, the while expert fingers explored her midriff and ribs.

'I can't take my eyes off you for a moment, can I?' demanded Guy. 'When I do you either get yourself robbed or try to break your neck. Why couldn't you just swim? Why had you to show off your no doubt Olympic prowess here, of all places?'

'I want to be sick,' Margot said miserably.

'No, you don't! In a minute or two you'll feel fine. Stand up! I want to make sure you still can.'

Margot stood up and her legs trembled. The skin on her thighs was sore and reddening from the impact of the water. In a way she was relieved, but confounded both herself and him by starting to cry.

'Here!' Guy gathered her up and marched over the rocks round the bluff of the cliff. 'Don't do that. We're supposed to be enjoying ourselves.'

'How can I w-when you're so r-rotten to me?' she sobbed.

'Rotten? Me? I don't know what you're talking about.' He set her down and thrust a towel at her. 'Now get dressed and we'll have lunch.'

She found she was hungry as she joined him and he handed her a fried chicken leg and a roll of delicious bread and uncorked a bottle of red, unlabelled, obviously local wine. The chicken was followed by a creamy cheese and another roll.

'Goat, but delicious,' Guy said, indicating the cheese. 'The gift of a grateful patient.' He filled up the tumbler holding her wine and she began to feel vaguely far away, like a character in a dream she was having.

He took out large rosy peaches and grimaced as he peeled one for her, the juice running over the napkin he held it in.

'One shouldn't really, but as a doctor I must insist. There! You'll enjoy that.' She did, and as she sipped at her third glass of wine felt even more strange. She lay down with the peach only half finished and closed her eyes. She could hardly open them to behold him leaning over her.

'I do believe you've had too much wine, I forgot you're not used to it. Go to sleep, then.' He lifted her head and cushioned it in the pullover he had simply tied round his neck in the car. Then there was only the sound of the sea in the silence, and the cliff overhang making a shadow from the hot sun over them both as they took a welcome siesta in these most natural of surroundings.

Margot awoke with a cry, though she didn't know of what she had been dreaming. She stood up feeling her ribs and abdomen gingerly, for she was now very sore and bruised.

'Guy?' she called, not seeing him near, and walked round the bluff. He was standing gazing out to sea, where a tourist ship was on its way to the island of Elba. She touched him and he whirled around as though attacked and prepared to strike back.

'It's only me,' she said soothingly. 'Who were you expecting?'

He frowned. 'I don't know. I was day-dreaming. Once, a long time ago, I came upon a fellow with a knife on a lonely beach like this. I suppose subconsciously I half expect to see him again. What's the matter? Sore tummy?'

'Yes.' She was rubbing hard. 'But that was only to be expected, I suppose, after what I did. I expect I'll live.'

'You should really have an X-ray taken, to make sure you haven't cracked a rib. Arrange it through Agostini. Margot, I've taken over the Whitham family, but I can't be your doctor. You must put yourself on Giulio's list.'

'But why——?' She was genuinely puzzled and then she saw his handsome countenance twisted in a kind of torment.

'Because, after the other night, I can't regard you as dispassionately as a doctor should. You know the rules. Ever since I first laid eyes on you you've churned me up so that I don't know whether I'm coming or going when you're around. I'm not a monk; I'm thirty-three years old and normally sexed, and when I kissed you the other evening I realised I was kissing a very attractive and responsive woman. I suppose we've both had our thoughts about what happened since then. At least, I have.'

She gasped. 'Oh, Guy, and so have I! I thought it was you who'd forgotten. Today you've kept me at such a distance that I was beginning to feel you'd regretted what happened and didn't want to continue. I was feeling quite miserable about it because a woman can't—doesn't—take the initiative in these things. You see, I'm attracted to you, too.'

The words were no sooner out of her mouth than he seized her almost roughly and kissed her. She knew that when he put her aside the attraction would only be deepened, that it was something of the mind and spirit as well as purely physical. When their lips parted she still clung to him breathlessly listening to the thud of his heart which seemed to echo the wild beating of her own.

'You see? You're a bad influence,' he told her, suddenly holding her off and smiling ruefully. 'The talking was supposed to come first.'

'The talking?' she echoed. 'What is there to say? I love you! I love you! I love you! There, I've said my say.'

'No, you mustn't! No, you can't! No, you don't! Not until I've had *my* say,' he said firmly. 'Now, come on. While I'm still in reasonable possession of my judgment we'd better get the car up to the road. I know a place where the Signora makes a good cup of English tea. We'll talk there, then we have to get back home. I'm taking evening surgery.'

Margot felt slightly mystified as the car whined in low gear up the ravine-like track from what she would always think of as their beach from now on. But what could words do to suppress emotions which were now running rampant between them, which made her reach out and touch his shoulder just to feel the thrill of communion again, and view the cliff road with hills on one side and the tossing sea on the other, through eyes renewed by recent events into scenes of beauty?

Once more Guy turned off into a rocky track which this time led to what appeared to be a typical Tuscan farmhouse, with goats and long-horned sheep grazing together on little scrubby hillocks, and an orchard behind the house full of olive trees and lemons in fragrant blossom and apples already large, oblong and green. But Signora Fattorini had gone into business on her own as a sideline, and there were several umbrellas on a well-scrubbed patio with tables below them, and the woman came out full of greetings for Guy and friendly curiosity regarding his companion.

'We're old friends,' Guy said, as the woman went to prepare the order of English tea and Italian home-made pastries. 'I was called to see her son, who had a perforated appendix. It was a near thing. I drove him into Siena myself, when the ambulance people were on strike, but now he's fully recovered and has gone up to Turin to be apprenticed in the car industry. She says he wouldn't be a farmer for anything and that as it's such hard work for her husband they're looking for a buyer for the property. They could build six modern villas on the place, she just told me.'

Margot grimaced. 'It's so lovely as it is. So peaceful and—and natural. What happens when all the farmers have gone? Who will grow food to feed the people in the villas?'

'Ah, sweet Margot! Who knows? Who knows?'

Signora Fattorini reappeared with a large tray. She set out the cups and saucers and plates and then said to Margot, 'Milk in first. That is English. Milk in first.'

'Yes, yes. Very good,' Margot smiled.

'Well done!' acknowledged Guy, putting a macaroon whole into his mouth. The woman laughed and chattered for a while to Guy and then made her way back into the house. Margot wondered, as silence fell between them, what the talking was to be about.

'Well?' she asked at length, as Guy disposed of another macaroon. 'What deep dark secrets are you going to reveal to me?'

'None, my darling. I just can't marry you.'

Margot felt as though she had been slapped in the face

with a wet towel. Her head rocked back with shock.

'It—it's early days to talk of marriage,' she said, her voice wobbling, 'but why not? Your wife died, I know. Is her memory sacred, then, or something? Would she want you never to marry again?'

'It's nothing to do with my wife,' he said quietly. 'I just can't get married to anyone. I don't want to talk about it—and don't you ever discuss us with Maxine.'

She poured the tea in trembling silence and passed him a cup.

'Oh, Guy, don't fool around, please! If I'm not allowed to talk about a subject which is obviously important to my future, if not to the present, may I ask what sort of relationship you propose we do have in its place?'

He sighed. 'I don't know, Margot. I honestly don't know. It would be easy if you were an attractive grass widow having a holiday away from her husband, whose sights were set on enjoying herself during the next two weeks or so; or even if you were a good-time girl who knew her way around in these matters and was looking for another scalp to add to her collection.'

He shrugged. 'But you're not the sort of girl to be happy as a partner in a casual affair. You should be some man's adored wife. It's your obvious destiny. But how can I, having held you in my arms, now let you go? I never thought of myself as doing such a juvenile thing as falling in love. Help me, Margot!'

She reached out and seized one of his hands in her own.

'How can I help either of us, Guy? I don't know why we can't marry—why you won't discuss it, but I'll accept your word for it. But what does that leave us?' Her eyes took on the dark grey of dove's wings as she groped for a solution.

He saw the sudden scarlet flush in her cheeks and her eyes falter before his. Now her lashes lay against her cheeks and it was he who squeezed her fingers reassuringly.

'You don't have to try to follow in the footsteps of others, my darling,' he said gently. 'I'm as much in the dark as you as to how our mutual destiny will work out. I want to be allowed to go on being in love with you, and whatever stems from that will be, I have no doubt. *Che sarà, sarà.* You know what that means. All we can be sure of is that we must say goodbye, probably when sweet is sweetest, maybe at the end of the summer.'

'But why, Guy?' she pleaded with all the eloquence of her fine eyes. 'A nurse can usually get work somewhere. My Italian should be fair by then, and there are hospitals——'

'I'm not intending to stay here much longer myself, Margot. I had plans to move on, before you came. I would rather say goodbye, here and now, than lead you on with false hopes which would eventually destroy us both and that we hold most dear.'

She was silent for some time.

'I—I only know I—can't say goodbye. I'd rather do it hating you than loving you. Not that I could ever hate you,' she added hastily.

'It's not really very happy, being in love like this, is it?' he asked her, putting her fingers gently to his lips and then stroking her hand, which looked so small and white in his large bronzed one.

'Well,' she smiled bravely, 'we must do something

about that. We have the summer—that's something. I'm not going to think about the goodbye part until I have to.'

'You're a gem, Margot. A gem among women. Let's eat up, for the Signora's sake, and then hurry away so that I have time to kiss you before I must leave you. I'm never going to be able to see enough of you.'

CHAPTER SIX

THERE seemed to be constant developments on all fronts during the next few weeks. Tourists now crammed all the resorts and Ricci was kept busy for a good deal of the time showing parties round the ruins and, no doubt, buying his supplies of candles wholesale to keep going a ritual which was no longer sanctified by the Mother of churches. But Margot felt quite friendly towards young Ricci in that he became George's first friend of his own age since his accident, and was therefore responsible for doing the invalid a whole lot of good. At George's invitation he came to the Villa Romana and chatted for a whole afternoon, and after that George wanted to see the ruins of the Terracini estate, and Ricci came to help Margot get him there.

On that afternoon, hot as it was, Ricci had set up his target and soon had George firing arrows with deepening enthusiasm for the sport. Sophia arrived, and the laughter of young people rang out in that ancient arena. Though Margot smiled she could no longer feel herself a part of youth, with its exuberance and innocence.

In an aura of otherworldness, Margot dutifully did her job, noting how much happier her employers and their family now were, since George had decided to endure what could not be cured.

He now had a law tutor, who normally lectured at a university of international fame, but was now on a working vacation. Mr Ewart was middle-aged and an ascetic-looking Scot, who had seen John Whitham's advertisement in a Rome newspaper and offered his services as coach. He lived at the local hostelry and required George's attention for five hours daily, three in the morning and two, from four until six, in the early evening. What with now having friends, and work to do, George was suddenly and surprisingly happy, and, as is always the case, he improved physically: his skin hardened from outdoor excursions; once he even got sunburnt when, having asked to be put in shorts, he spent too long at archery on a hot afternoon in the sun. Margot blamed herself for that, for though George was paralysed from the waist down, such people are still aware of pain in their lower extremities, and George suffered as his thighs burned, even though his nurse gently applied calamine lotion.

'George,' she suggested, 'wear slacks until we get your legs used to the sun. Once you're better we'll give you a little sun each day until you toughen up. O.K.?'

'O.K.,' he agreed. 'I may toughen up faster with some sea swimming. Ricci says there's a private bay down below, where the Terracini family used to bathe, and that it's sandy and quiet. He suggests we all go swimming there some Sunday. That's his day off. Any objections, Nurse?'

'No. That is if you decide not to swim out to sea where

I can't follow you. I don't want any more swimming jokes played on me.'

'Fair enough. Anyway, Ricci's a good swimmer. He could always haul me back.'

'You like Ricci, don't you?' asked Margot.

'Yes—I like him as a pal. I wouldn't want him going after Tessa, or anything like that.'

'Why not?'

'Well, he has Latin lover pretensions, I would say,' George said soberly. 'He was telling me that some of his friends—the good-looking ones—live off older women quite successfully. They learn pretty manners and are kept like lapdogs. He didn't seem to think that was so awful.'

'Well, *I* think it's terrible. Could you be somebody's lapdog, George?'

'You kidding? With my face, which has been likened to a bull terrier's? But Ricci's handsome——'

She shrugged. 'I suppose he is. I think he's effeminate, bleaching his hair and all that.'

'You just got to be kidding now, Nurse. Ricci likes women.'

'But I thought their girls were kept like nuns?'

'Oh, not Italian girls. Tourists. The permissive society has brought its dubious benefits to the Riccis of this world. I do believe I've shocked you, Nurse! Wonders will never cease! Has he ever made a pass at you—like that?'

She remembered how it had felt in the cave with the Italian and shuddered inwardly.

'No, he hasn't,' she said quickly. 'But he does see

rather a lot of young Sophia. If he's like that shouldn't we warn her?'

'Maybe there's no need. He told me that young Sophia's got a bit of a crush on him and can be a nuisance.'

'I like Master Ricci Lamati rather less than I did ten minutes ago. I hope he's not a bad influence on you.'

'I suppose I'm stuck with what I am by now,' said George. 'Ricci's O.K. Maybe what he told me was braggadocio; guys do talk like that among themselves. I don't suppose he's any exception.'

The next Thursday Guy was waiting at the gate, as usual, with the car, and refused to say where they were going. Margot saw the picnic hamper on the back seat.

'Doesn't your sister mind packing food for other people?' she asked, after the car had stopped a couple of hundred yards further on for them to exchange a breathless good-morning kiss. 'I think I should provide the picnic sometimes.'

'Maxine loves doing it. She likes to make people happy.'

'But what about her? Isn't she lonely?'

'Not at all. She has the Land-rover in case she wants to go marketing or trying on dresses, but she's at her happiest in a kitchen. She likes cooking.'

'That's nice for you. I doubt I could do more than boil an egg. I think your sister is very pretty.'

'Oh, she is. She grew up with people telling her how beautiful she was. That's why the accident was such a traumatic experience for her.'

'The accident?'

Guy smiled. 'You didn't notice the scar tissue on her nose and left cheek? Oh, that's good! She's getting very clever with make-up. She wasn't wearing a safety-belt and went flying through a windscreen. Her face was cut to ribbons. Even one eye was badly cut. It took years and many operations, but even I, looking at her, sometimes forget, such a good job the surgeons did.'

'Do you think she minds about you and me?'

'Maxine doesn't mind about me and anybody. Oh, I'm sorry—that makes it all sound too general, as though I spend every summer with a different girl.'

'And don't you?' she asked.

'If I've given you the impression that you're just one in a crowd, Margot, I'll turn the car round and take you back home. Have I? Be honest!'

'No. No, you haven't. I'm sorry, Guy. I suppose loving somebody makes one touchy. You've been very frank with me and I've told you about Mike. But this *is* different, isn't it, Guy?'

'It's a butterfly, Margot. Leave it alone and it's beautiful and fragile and a joy to behold. Catch it in your hand to examine it and it's out of its element. It dies.'

Guy knew the coast intimately. He now sought out a small fishing village with a natural harbour where about a dozen fishing trawlers lay at rest. Obviouly Aventura was cashing in on the tourist industry. A few pallid bodies were laid out on towels near the harbour wall. A *pensione* was obviously full of visitors, judging from the towels and beachwear hanging from the windows, and a half-built hotel was going up on the hill behind the village.

The car was parked, locked, and everything portable

removed from it, then a small boy was adjured to guard it faithfully.

'That's Rodolfo,' Guy explained, 'another of my ex-patients. His married sister lives in Astria. Come on!'

'Where are we going?' Margot asked in delight as she was hustled along a kind of mole reaching into the sea. 'I have a feeling I'm being abducted, and I like it.'

'I hope you do.' Guy stopped and dumped the picnic basket as he waved towards a blue boat bobbing in the water by a small flight of stone steps. 'There she is, the *Aphrodite*.'

'I can only see the number fifty-one painted on her,' Margot said in puzzlement.

'Well, to me she's *Aphrodite*,' responded Guy. 'The fellow who owned her capsized her in a gale and she was literally dragged from the waters, just like her namesake. Do you like her?'

'Isn't she a bit small?' Margot asked.

'Plenty big enough for two, I assure you, and I'm not asking anybody else along. I'll do the driving and you can be crew. That's after we get the sail up. She's a sailing dinghy. Don't tell me you're a landlubber, darling?'

'It's that bit about capsizing in a gale. Couldn't she do it again?'

'Don't worry, I've informed the harbour master where we're going and when to start an air-sea rescue search.'

'You're teasing me!' she exclaimed.

'And *you're* scared. Now are you going to take that small step for mankind on board, or do we forget it?'

'I'm going on board.' She hesitated to tell him that she had never been on any kind of a boat in her life. She didn't know what sort of sailor she would prove to be—

one who laughed and leapt about in the teeth of the elements or hung miserably over the side being sick. The craft seemed so fragile and wobbled as she stepped aboard and more so as Guy joined her and dumped the picnic basket. He told her where to sit to give the dinghy the proper trim, and, seeing her flower-like pale and uncertain face pointed to a rope which she was to place around her person.

'I don't want to lose you,' he smiled reassuringly. 'Don't worry, I know what I'm doing.'

He untied the dinghy from the dockside and it drifted out a few yards before he hoisted the mainsail and then the jib, which he tied down as the breeze caught them and bowled them out beyond the mole and into open water.

'Oh, I like it! I like it!' Margot cried out in exhilaration.

'Good!' said Guy, from the tiller. 'In the locker to your right there's a life-jacket. Put it on.'

'But why? The weather's perfect.'

'I know, but it's a rule of the local Yacht Club. Life-jackets to be worn or I lose my insurance if anything happens. Chuck the other one from the opposite locker to me.'

Apart from ducking her head when the jib-boom came over, Margot didn't move for the next hour. She watched the coastline fade into a heat haze and saw the sea glistening all about, in shades of royal blue lightening to turquoise, depending on the depth of the sea-bed hereabouts. There were a few other sailing craft about and once a motor cruiser which set them bobbing in its wake. Then a rocky island loomed up from which rose clouds of sea-birds, noisy and quarrelsome and busy about their own everyday affairs.

'What's that?' asked Margot.

'It's called Eden, a bird sanctuary. Fortunately we're allowed to land providing we're not under power. The conservationists don't want the birds to be frightened away by the phut-phutting of motors.'

The boom swung over as they rounded the island. Facing the open sea was a small sandy cove and to one side of it a deep pool enclosed by rocks into which had been carved steps.

'It looks as if we have the place to ourselves,' Guy said, in obvious delight. 'That is apart from nature's inhabitants.'

He quickly furled down the sails and the *Aphrodite* glided into the basin, where Guy was quick to tie her up to an iron ring let into the rock.

'You can take your life-jacket off now, darling,' he said, as he staggered up the steps with the picnic basket, which he dumped and then came back to give his companion a hand.

'Welcome to Eden,' he said, looking deeply and meaningfully into her questioning eyes. 'I'm almost sorry I can't guarantee an apple-tree.'

Margot flushed and laughed as the implication of his words sank home.

'As if you need one!' she told him, as she jumped lightly to the warm-baked sand and walked a little in advance of him. 'You, who once told me you took what you wanted from women! Where are we going?'

'Just over there where we can lie on grass. The sand gets very hot. We'll sunbathe for a while, then have a swim and our meal, in that order. To explore the island disturbs the birds, and I only brought you here to be alone with you. I hope you don't mind. Wherever we've gone, previously, there have been other people or the possibility of people. I thought that would be best.'

Though she took deep breaths Margot still felt peculiarly breathless, with her heartbeat doing overtime. It must feel like this to be half-way up Everest with the air growing rarefied, and yet they were here at sea-level and Guy was putting down large beach towels for them to lie on. A flock of—could they be gannets?—flew overhead to investigate and, feeling no threat to themselves, squawked off over the headland. A painted ship on a painted ocean passed a mile or so out to sea; it had red sails and a striped spinnaker, full blown.

'How can you get a suntan in a dress?' he asked. 'Aren't you wearing your swimsuit?'

She took off her dress and he regarded her trim figure in the swimsuit speculatively.

'Pretty,' he decided. 'I mean what's in it, too.' He drew her to him. She did not even know why it was she trembled when her whole body was so eager to submit to his masculine demands; she had never felt like this with anyone else in her life; never known this desire to merge, or felt that perhaps she was only half of an entity magnetised by the wholeness another person could make of her.

But she was not unwilling to learn and it was only when Guy pushed her firmly away from him that through the thunder of emotions aroused within her she heard the shrill of Italian voices and realised they were no longer alone in their Eden. Still breathing with the same difficulty she had experienced earlier, she saw what appeared to be a family party pulling a large flat-bottomed rowing boat up on to the beach.

'Let's go and swim,' said Guy. She followed him down to the water's edge, hearing him exchange pleasantries with the newcomers. The water was surprisingly chill after the heat of past moments. She gasped and struck out and then lay on her back and looked at the blue bowl of the sky with only one cloud, apparently made out of white lawn, shaping itself into a question mark as she watched.

Guy swam up to her.

'You know, my love, cold water is wonderful for bringing the temperature down? We refrigerate patients, sometimes, for their own good. When you can promise not to seduce me, which you very nearly did a little while ago, then come out and get dry and dressed. We'll eat, protected as we are by other company, and then we'll set sail for home again. And never—never, I insist—will I put myself on a desert island with you again. You witch!'

He began to walk through the shallows.

'Guy!'

He turned and blew her a silent kiss. 'I mean it,' he told her, and walked off up the beach. Margot tried to focus on the cloud, but little by little it was disintegrating. She felt a kind of accord with it, as though she, too, would never be quite the same ever again.

The sun had dried them and they had lunched in silence, more than made up for by the Italian party, who had spread themselves out on the beach and all seemed to be talking, or rather shouting at once. The two younger children were investigating the *Aphrodite* and their mother, large, fat, black-glossy haired, yelled in a loud crescendo above the rest; '*Avanti*, Cesare, Sergio! *Avanti! Avanti!*'

Margot slipped on her demure little dress and remained kneeling. She pulled a comb through her hair which danced with health.

'We can't go on like this, you know,' she murmured at length. 'Or rather, like—like that. The way we were.'

'I agree entirely,' said Guy, pulling his shirt on loosely and taking slivers of dried grass from the collar. 'Next time we must go for culture; museums, concerts, things like that.'

'Oh, you just don't seem to understand! It was all so right, so natural. We ought to be married.' She felt the warning flash of his glance rather than saw it and added, 'I know we can't marry. You made all that quite clear before we really got started. I'm not complaining—it's just that I can't feel platonically about you.'

'Nor I about you, my sweet.' He glanced at her from under assessing lids. 'I don't know whether you're going to believe this or not, Margot, but I really didn't bring you here to take advantage of you. What happened took us both a bit out of our depth. We are obviously flint and tinder, or whatever. I don't know. Words are a poor substitute for the experience. I can only promise that I won't do it again.'

She sank a little dejectedly into herself. 'At least,' he continued, 'not until we know each other a good deal better. There *are* other aspects to a relationship, you know. We've been inclined to dwell on one, which mustn't be allowed to assume all importance. How do you know you would even like me afterwards? You won't, not unless you learn to like me before. So we *are* going to museums and concerts.'

The sail back took longer, as the breeze was off the land and Guy had to tack to make any way at all. For the whole two and a half hours Margot sat quietly in her life-jacket, ducking obediently when told, enjoying the delight of watching Guy always busy, studying the sky and watching for any movement in the sails, and then Aventura was ahead with its reaching mole and enclosed little harbour.

'I can't see you tomorrow night,' Guy announced as he tied the boat up and helped her to alight. 'I'm going to see a friend in hospital in Siena.'

She tried to hide her disappointment. 'It's not because of——?' she began to ask as they walked along the mole towards the Alfa Romeo.

'It's because I have to see this friend in hospital, my sweet. The following evening we'll take Teresa for a lovely long walk. I'll be waiting for you after your lesson at Miss MacDougal's. How are you getting on, by the way?'

'Not too badly. While we're walking Teresa you can ask me some irregular verbs.'

When Margot rang at the Villa Romana to be admitted, Salvatore stayed her and went to his own quarters to bring her a hand-written letter addressed to her, but unstamped. It was faintly perfumed and she was puzzled as she went off to her room to open it. She withdrew a deckle-edged sheet of paper from the envelope and read. It was headed 'Villa Fiorita', Guy's address, and was from his sister.

'Dear Nurse Walsh,

'My brother has to go out tomorrow evening and I would appreciate the pleasure of your company at my otherwise solitary dinner table. We are more or less the same generation and I am sure would enjoy a good gossip together. I'm told my cooking isn't too bad, either, so I will take your silence to mean consent if I don't hear from you to the contrary by nine this evening.'

Margot glanced at her watch and it was half-past nine. Guy had driven the long way home through the hills of the hinterland.

'Don't dress too formally, and I shall hope to see you at eight-thirty for nine. Hoping most sincerely to see you,

Yours,

Maxine Derwent.'

Margot's first reaction was blind panic. She didn't know what Maxine's motive was in wanting to see her, and did not quite believe it was simply one woman's desire to gossip with another. Maxine knew that her twin brother took her out; she even packed picnics for them and had done that very day; that almost-fateful, ever-to-be-remembered day, when what had once been termed honour had almost been forfeited to the demands of urgent and blind, unreasoning need. What did Maxine imagine went on during such expeditions? Would she have approved? Did she really, in her heart, know? Had it all the ring of familiarity about it for her?

Margot didn't particularly want to go and have dinner with Guy's sister, but how could she avoid it without appearing rude? Maybe George could have a convenient relapse and so provide an excuse.

'No, I didn't mean that!' Margot said quickly, in case there really was Someone who always listened to one's heart. 'I want George to keep on improving, both mentally and physically, and I'll go and have dinner with Maxine. It's not such an ordeal, surely?'

Every Friday Margot had the same feeling of disorientation as she went about her everyday tasks. It was rather as though all her living concentrated into those days she spent with Guy, and other days she merely existed. They were like the dashes authors used between powerful sentences, simply there to lend weight to the substance.

Yet she quite enjoyed her days at the Villa Romana, too, watching as her patient achieved more and more independence and learned to live with his disability.

On this day she was not very happy to see Ricci lounging by the swimming pool as she accompanied George for his daily exercise.

'Did you say he could come here?' she asked George.

'No, I didn't, but let's be hospitable, eh, Nurse?'

Ricci approached and gave her a little bow, then gripped George's hand in welcome.

'Good morning! Good morning! The book I promised you, my friend.'

'Thanks, Ricci.'

'Now I will go.'

'No—come on and have a swim first.'

Margot thought it a little too coincidental that Ricci was wearing swimming trunks under his slacks, which he slipped off unselfconsciously.

'No tours today, Ricci?' she asked conversationally.

'Yes, I have a tour at eleven. But I think there is plenty of time?'

Margot tried not to feel mean, especially when the Italian said, 'I help you, George? Come on.' His own body was like that of a Roman sculpture and his muscles, though slight, hardened into steel as he took George's weight and helped to lower him into the water.

'Well, hello!' Tessa had arrived, unnoticed, and was looking Ricci up and down. 'I've heard about you. You're George's friend.'

When the three were in the pool, racing each other and laughing, Margot went back to the house to tidy up George's room. It was easier to go in by the front entrance, as she hadn't George with her, and she noticed an argument going on at the main gate between Lucia, one of the daily maids, and a peasant woman all in black, her skin wrinkled and aged before her time. Lucia was trying to close the gate but the woman was arguing angrily. The girl was the only member of the staff who knew some English, and Margot went to see if she could be of any assistance.

'What's the matter, Lucia?'

'Oh, *signorina*, some mistake. This ignorant woman is saying she wants to see her son, that he has some money for her. But I have told her there's no member of the staff here of his name. She was just saying, when you arrived, that her son is not on our staff, that he is visiting. But I tell her there are no visitors here.'

'Oh, but there is one, Lucia. He's swimming in the pool with Master George and Miss Tessa.'

'But how can that be, *signorina*? Salvatore is sick to

his stomach this morning, and nobody has come to the gate until now. I have let no one in, I swear.'

Margot looked at the high walls and the solid oak-studded gates and realised they were too much, even for Ricci. But for one who could disappear over a cliff, as he had done, to discover a subterranean chamber, then the wall which guarded the Villa Romana from the cliff-edge at the bottom of the grounds might not present insurmountable problems.

'What is the *signora*'s name?' Margot asked.

'Frascati. But she says her son was by an earlier marriage and is named Lamati—Riccardo Alfredo Lamati.'

'Then he *is* here,' said Margot. 'I'll go and tell him his mother is waiting to see him.'

'But how——? I haven't opened the gates until now, *signorina*.'

'Maybe the tradesman's entrance?'

'No. Giovanna keeps the key to that and she is marketing in the village. I saw her lock the door after her.'

'Then perhaps you would like to ask Ricci Lamati how he got in when he comes, Lucia? Meanwhile take Signora Frascati round to the kitchen and give the poor thing a drink of something. She looks tired and her feet seem to be hurting.'

Margot returned to the pool to find Ricci just emerging and borrowing a towel from the heap always kept available.

'Oh, Ricci,' she hesitated, 'a Signora Frascati is asking for you. She's in the kitchen with our maid, Lucia.'

'Signora Frascati is here?' For a moment Ricci looked hunted and then he flashed one of his ready smiles. 'Oh! I wonder what she wants with me? One of our servants from home,' he told Tessa, who was within earshot. He pulled on his slacks and a loose floral shirt and saluted George, who was still swimming up and down the pool energetically.

'See you all soon, then,' he called, and ran off towards the house.

'He's nice, isn't he?' asked Tessa.

'He's nice,' Margot agreed, wondering how nice a young man was who denied his own mother. The more she thought about it the more she wondered whether Ricci was really a medical student at all, or just a boy from the gutter who pulled himself up by means of accomplished lies. There was no shame in being poor, providing that one was honest, but the more she saw of Ricci Lamati the more she had to remind herself of the philosophy of the three wise monkeys. Charm could disguise so many flaws in the human character.

'What's this about seeing him soon?' she asked Tessa, seeing that George was at last tiring and indicating that this was his last length.

'Oh, we're all going down to some beach—you, me, Ricci, George and Sophia Lindsay. Ricci is going to build a fire and cook some whitebait for us. George can swim in the sea. Van can come if he wants, but if he does he'll only be poking about in rock-pools. Now I'm famished. I hope brunch is ready.'

Lithe and beautiful, Tessa wrapped a shapeless towel around her and made off while Margot called for Enrico, who she knew wasn't far off by the disgusting smell of the cheap cigarettes he smoked.

She went quickly when she heard the 'brunch' party breaking up; she herself was an early breakfaster and

usually took a salad and cheese lunch on a tray either in
her room or the garden. George wanted a nap and his
tutor was coming for two hours in the afternoon, so Margot
gave him a quick talcum rub and saw him settled and
then took a book to her own room to read, but it was so
hot nowadays by noon that even the buzzing of a blue-
bottle could put one in a drowsy state and make all the
words on a page slip together.

She looked up and out at the sea, sequin-specked and
eye-achingly brilliant. It was no good. She had to put
down her book and lie on the bed. As she entered the
arm of Morpheus Guy took over and led her across
Elysian fields where there was no end to eternal summer and no repenting of love.

When we dream of such enchantments, waking up can
bring only cares and confusion, and then, if we are wise,
commonsense takes over and we meet life on its own
terms. So Margot washed the sleep and the dreams from
her eyes and told herself she had a job to do, and sailed
forth and did it.

CHAPTER SEVEN

MARGOT rang the bell at the Villa Fiorita feeling
strangely nervous at the idea of being tête-à-tête with
Guy's twin sister. Maxine opened the door herself and
smiled under the shaded porch-light.

'Good!' she exclaimed. 'I'm so glad that you could
come. I've sent the maid home, because I like to do the

cooking, and as there are just the two of us I thought we could manage.'

'You must let me help where I can,' said Margot, taking her hostess's outstretched hand, 'such as clearing away and washing up.'

'Oh, you can come again,' Maxine laughed, leading the way indoors. The lights were all subdued; in the dining-room there was only candlelight from tall red candles in silver candelabra. 'How about an aperitif?'

'Oh, you go ahead, please,' smiled Margot. 'I see we're having wine with our meal, so I won't, if you don't mind. I haven't a great deal of tolerance to alcohol.'

'Well, we'll just start, shall we? I like your dress, Nurse Walsh.'

Margot was wearing a green dress which was mid-calf length and with a short bolero jacket to match.

'Thank you. But please call me Margot.'

'Right, I will. And I'm Maxine.' She disappeared and returned with the first course, fat prawns in salad. It was more than a cocktail, more like a dish. 'Do sit down, Margot.'

'You're not really alike for twins, are you?' Margot said for the sake of making conversation at this point. 'Not that twins of different sexes are identical, ever, but sometimes the relationship is obvious.'

'We're more alike than we appear at the moment. I dye my hair.' Margot didn't comment and Maxine proceeded, 'I wish I hadn't started it now, as it becomes so brassy in time. My natural hair is brown, but if it had been as dark as Guy's I might have left it alone. Even now I keep trying to pluck up the courage to let it grow out.'

'You could have a short, shaped cut and a rinse, couldn't you?' asked Margot.

'My dear, I tried that! The rinse made me orange. I hid away for two weeks, but Guy, who did see me, just never stopped laughing.' She smiled in reminiscence.

'This is delicious,' Margot commented. 'I didn't realise how hungry I was.'

'We're having stuffed roast pork for our main course —Guy will kick himself for missing it—with new potatoes and baby peas. Ready?'

'More than ready. No——' as Maxine reached out for her dish—'let me clear away and carry through. You've had all the trouble of preparing and cooking.'

The kitchen was small but seemed very well organised.

'Just dump those in the sink,' said Maxine. 'The pleasure of eating comes first. Would you like to take the vegetables through and open the wine?'

No sooner had Margot filled glasses with the sparkling Italian wine than Maxine appeared with the meat on two plates.

'I carved through there. It's such a messy job at table. I must say Guy's very good at carving, but women are inclined to tear at meat.'

'That looks absolutely gorgeous,' said Margot, helping herself to vegetables. 'How do you make the stuffing?'

'Well, that's a secret, actually——'

'Oh, I'm sorry. I didn't mean——'

'No, I don't mean it's a personal secret. What I really meant was it's my own special makeshift. One can't always get decent cooking apples here, and so I experimented until I found what was an ideal sweet and sour stuffing. It has a basis of chopped salami and garlic, apricots, walnuts and olives, and has proved so popular that now I don't bother with apples even when they're in season. What do you think?'

'I heard you were a good cook, and I thoroughly endorse it. It's delicious.'

'You must store the recipe in your noddle for when you get married, Margot. Are you engaged—or anything?'

'No. Nothing.'

'Do I detect a note of wistfulness there? Would you like to get married?'

'I think it's at the back of every woman's mind, even the so-called liberated ones.'

'If it works out marriage can be heaven,' nodded Maxine, 'but it can go the other way. What do you think of my brother?'

'How—how do you mean?'

'Well, is he attractive, do you think?'

'I—I suppose he is. But we were talking of marriage, and your brother doesn't go around asking every girl he meets to marry him.'

'Would you marry Guy, if you could?'

Margot actually choked and was flushed when she had finished coughing. 'Maxine, that's not a fair question, is it? If it did arise it would be a matter between Guy and me. But it hasn't arisen, if that's what you really wanted to know.'

'Oh, dear, now I've offended you. I suppose it did sound as though I was trying to ferret information out of you. You can't blame me for being interested in my brother's welfare, though, can you? Not when we were born within half an hour of each other and have shared simply everything together? I naturally wonder what's driving him away from Astria. He's suddenly decided to accept the offer of a job in Venezuela, and expects me to go along with him, and of course I shan't let him down. I'll accompany him. But I did think that perhaps the decision had something to do with you.'

'I don't think I understand. Why me?'

'Well, he might have fallen in love with you, really madly, and felt he couldn't marry you and so ought to go away ...'

Margot remembered Guy's urging her not to discuss their relationship with his sister, but this was easier said than done.

'Obviously I can't be expected to know why your brother feels he can't marry,' she said, 'because I think it's the right of people who really love each other and want to be together to marry if they want to——'

'Oh, I couldn't agree more!' Maxine interrupted.

'——but as I'm expecting to leave Italy at the end of the summer, now that my patient is so much improved, I don't think Guy is going to Venezuela to get away from me.' She remembered wryly how she had suggested getting a hospital job and staying on, and that Guy had told her he himself was leaving Italy. 'No, it's nothing to do with me,' she said with greater emphasis.

'Oh, I hope it's not *her*. Not *that* woman!' Maxine said suddenly, automatically scooping more peas on to Margot's plate.

'Which woman are we talking about?' Margot asked.

Without immediately answering the question Maxine

said, 'There's something happened to Guy, I know, and quite recently. Being a twin makes one much more observant. At times he's almost too happy to be true, and then he'll have a mood, a bad mood, and will snap if I ask what's up. I know he's a perfectly normal man who should have a woman by his side, and I don't mean it should be his sister.' She looked frankly at Margot. 'I thought he'd fallen in love with you. That's why I asked you here, to pump you, why I've encouraged him, packed you picnics. They *were* for you, weren't they?'

'Yes. We've had some lovely picnics. Thank you, very much.'

'Then what happened between you? It's because *she's* turned up again, when it was supposed to be all over. I've nearly had my ear bitten off when I've mentioned her name.'

'Whose name?' Margot persisted.

'Yvonne Mountstewart's—*Lady* Mountstewart, and a married woman. I think Guy was quite taken with her about two years ago, and then she told him that her marriage was drifting on to the rocks and that he might be interested in being named as co-respondent in a divorce case. Guy was upset, I know, but it seemed to end with him being miserable and her going off on somebody's yacht. He never wanted to discuss her until one day last week he quite casually mentioned that Yvonne was back in the family house near Leghorn. I asked if she was still married to Mountstewart, and he said yes, and laughed, and added that Yvonne liked being Lady Mountstewart too much to give it up lightly. Then two days ago he got this lavender-scented letter and told me Yvonne was in hospital and wanted to see him. He said he was going this evening and might be late back. I told him I was making my speciality—the roast pork—but he didn't even seem to hear. Now if that business all flared up again it could be a pretty kettle of fish; stinking fish, at that. Because she's just not the right person for Guy. I have this instinct and—and when I first met her I hated her on sight. I'll bet he's been seeing her secretly, knowing how I feel.'

Margot felt as though she had been slapped by a wet towel. Hearing like this about Guy's earlier romantic experiences was offensive, and now she viewed her own excursions with Guy in the light that they might not even be unique; to her, perhaps, but not to him. But then, he had never said that she had been the only woman in his life. It was only at times like yesterday, on the island whose Italian name was Eden, that she felt they were experiencing something rare and wonderful, that the two of them had something of value in their relationship.

'Are you all right, Margot?' asked Maxine. 'Is the food all right for you?'

'Yes. It's absolutely lovely. But far more than I eat normally.'

'And I talk too much, don't I? I've been poking and prying and digging at you and you've probably had a hard day's work and just want to relax. Could you manage a small helping of my lemon chiffon?'

'I don't think I could resist it. But please, just a small helping. No, *I'll* clear away, I insist. I haven't had a hard day's work. George is hardly any trouble, nowadays. I don't know whether your brother has told you, or not, but he used to be an absolute fiend.'

'Yes, Guy has mentioned the fact that your patient was running you ragged at one time, and that you needed a bit of relaxation away from him. He said he was going to get you out of that house by hook or by crook, and being Guy, he seems to have succeeded.'

Margot gave a wintry little smile as she scraped the scraps from the plates and then put all the soiled dishes to soak in hot soapy water before following her hostess back into the dining-room to eat the dessert. Maxine had paused by a wall-mirror, though in the candlelight she couldn't have seen very clearly.

'My God, my make-up's melting away! It *is* rather warm, isn't it?' She set down the dishes and shrugged prettily. 'It's so nice to be able to relax with someone who wouldn't be worried by my disfigurements.'

'What disfigurements?' Margot asked, having temporarily forgotten.

'I have a face like a cracked old plate. I got it in a motor accident.'

'Oh'—Margot genuinely peered—'there's hardly anything to see. You're very pretty, Maxine. I mean that.'

'I believe you do. How nice of you! You've made my evening. I already feel we're friends. Perhaps now we have met like this, we could meet again? I feel this— this empathy between us, which is most odd between women. Not all Guy's women friends are eager for my company, I can tell you. They seem to see me as a threat, and I suppose, up until now, I have been. May I explain?'

Margot felt that to say no would have severed any empathy that existed between them. Maxine was dying to get something off her chest and was in a mood now to do so. She went ahead without her guest uttering a single word.

'When you're a twin, you're close. You fight with your partner at times, of course, but you wouldn't let anybody else do so. This situation is peculiar to childhood in particular, because inevitably growing up brings other relationships which have to be accepted, although, at first, painfully.'

She smiled and continued, 'When Guy said he was getting married, I couldn't believe it. He was so young and seemed no different, though I had already been in love a couple of times and found the experiences crucifying. Well, Guy wasn't married for long. She died— maybe he's told you—but all that is history now. I fell in love with James, which I fancied was the love to end all loves. We married, and only six months later, after a silly row, he crashed the car and was killed. I was dragged from the wreckage praying to be allowed to die. My world had ended. They sent for Guy when they'd stitched me together, but my mind was still bleeding to death. I'd tried to take an overdose by only pretending to take my sleeping pills at night. When I thought I had enough I took the lot, but I woke up, and then they moved me to a psychiatric unit.

'I can't tell you the strength I drew from Guy. It was as though we'd gone back to our childhood and only needed each other. Guy told me that we would live together, that he would look after me. I asked him supposing he married again, what would happen to me then? He said he never would. He promised me. I seemed to get better quickly after that. I even learned that the terrible pain of loss gets better with time. I remember James, of course, but no longer with unhappiness. The dead, I think, must be allowed to go their way and we who are left must get on with our living. I kept house for Guy in a cottage near Ascot at first, and he was always there to encourage me as I kept having more and more cosmetic surgery. I had to have an eyebrow transplant, and my nose—which had been broken—had to be set twice. The result is as you see. I have to live with it now.'

'The result is very good,' Margot said.

'We came here about five years ago,' Maxine went on. 'As a family we seemed to be disaster-prone. Guy damaged his operating hand and the whole question of his career needed re-thinking. He worked first in a clinic near Rome, and then we discovered this place, and liked it, and so bought the villa. At first Guy stayed in Rome and came home for weekends, until he met Doctor Agostini, who had lost both his sons to higher-paid careers. They wanted more than merely being his partners in practice. Guy has had several affairs with women, but he's young and healthy and I didn't mind. I knew he would never desert me.'

Maxine sighed. 'Sometimes I thought that he had never really been in love, not as I was in love with James, and that he was still searching for it. I know now that when he married, his wife was already condemned to death. Pity is strong in Guy's make-up. He pitied her so much that it was a kind of love, and he pitied me in the mess I was in so that I battened on his love to make me better again. I hope I haven't bored you with all this, Margot, because so far I've been telling you our story up to date. Now, however, things could be different. I don't need Guy any longer, other than as my dearly-loved twin brother, which he will always be. If he fell in love and wanted to marry, I would rejoice, because, you see, the miracle has happened and I'm in love again myself.'

Margot looked at her sharply and questioningly.

'Yes, it's true. He's seen me often, in broad daylight, scars and all, and it doesn't seem to matter. It doesn't matter. I've made very sure, so sure that I haven't introduced Paolo to Guy yet.'

'So he's Italian?' Margot asked.

'Yes, but he speaks fluent English, which is just as well considering the state of my Italian!' Maxine stopped to laugh, and she was very pretty when she was gay. 'So you see now why I've been pumping you, hoping it was the same between you and Guy? We could have made it a double wedding.'

'And Venezuela?' Margot asked flatly.

'Yes, well, if Guy still wants to go I'll accompany him.'

'And Paolo?'

'Guy has made many sacrifices for me. Can I do less for him? Twins are special, you know. I intended introducing him to Paolo quite soon, but if he's involved again with that Mountstewart woman he may jump to her piping. I won't encourage him in that.'

'Don't you think, Maxine, that you should let him decide his own future?' Margot asked. 'You may be his twin, but that possibly means you're incapable of judging things dispassionately enough.'

'You think I should tell him about Paolo and me and then leave him to make his own decisions?'

'I certainly don't think you can make them for him by deciding whom he may or may not love.'

'You're probably wiser than I am. I'll think about things very carefully.'

'And now I really must go.' Margot looked at the clock in amazement. It was half-past midnight, and not only would she have to rouse poor old Salvatore to admit her to the Villa Romana, but Guy was out late too, and with another woman.

Maxine wouldn't hear of her helping to wash up.

'That job can wait for morning when the girl comes,' she said, helping Margot put a shawl round her shoulders against the night air. 'Thanks for coming. I have enjoyed our chat. Hark at me—*our* chat! I should say thanks for listening to the monologue. Maybe we can do it again, some time——?'

A car was coming down the road and Margot's heart-beat quickened. It was not the red Alfa Romeo but a large green Mercedes. It stopped at the Villa Fiorita and she heard Maxine's voice tremulous with excitement.

'Paolo, are you mad? At this hour? You *are* mad!'

The engine started up after a brief delay and for an instant Margot saw Maxine's countenance, absolutely entranced, pressed against the glass as it passed her. She waved and then she was not only alone, but lonely. She stood for fully five minutes outside the Villa Romana unable to bring herself to ring the bell and summon Salvatore. She wanted to weep, but the well of her tears was too deep and she couldn't reach it. Her eyes remained dry and felt hard and bright as the diamonds studding the sky. Perhaps, said hope, when she saw Guy tomorrow he would explain and all will be well. Perhaps it was all only a misunderstanding on her part: from deep happiness had come doubt so bitter that she could only question it.

What she could not question was Guy's insistence that she should not discuss their relationship with his sister, and he had been most emphatic on that point. It now looked to her as though he knew Maxine would probe and that she must remain no wiser after her probing. Yet if she could have told Maxine, 'Yes, I am in love with your brother, and he with me,' then some happy ending might well have been on the cards. Maxine had even mentioned a double wedding. Yet Guy had always insisted he could never marry. Always she came back to square one in her ponderings. It was like suddenly seeing through a glass, darkly, what had once reflected only brightness. It was like seeing the obverse of a coin which made it promptly unfamiliar to the eye. It was uncertainty and fear and an inner souring of all that had been sweetest. It was a kind of hell.

Fortunately Salvatore was half-asleep; he opened the gates automatically and scarcely responded to her apology and goodnight. She slid like a ghost to her room, for there were still people talking in the study. She undressed, showered and got into bed. At four in the morning she had still not slept.

Next day Margot felt not quite in the world, or of it. George, on the other hand, was very bright and talked almost non-stop as she attended to him.

'Cat got your tongue, Nurse?' he asked finally.

'No, but getting a word in edgeways hasn't been easy.'

'Oh, I thought you'd be interested in my plans for the

future. It was you who encouraged me to believe I had a future, wasn't it?'

'Of course I'm interested in all you do and plan, George. I'm really thrilled for you. You're going to law school and I'm sure you're going to do well. You're a very determined young man with a lot of guts.'

'I shall miss you,' he said suddenly.

'Miss me?'

George looked a little foolish and then said, with an odd laugh, 'Well, I can't take you to law school with me, can I? I'll have to look out for myself, I guess.'

'There'll be some sort of matron in the school, with nursing experience,' said Margot. 'You probably won't be the only young man there with—with difficulties. You'll be looked after. But you need so little doing for you now, anyway.'

'Yes, well—I really meant I'd miss *you*.'

'As I'll miss you,' Margot said sincerely. 'Gosh, George, you've been a handful, but it's been worth it. I've really enjoyed looking after you. But nothing stands still and we both have to move on.'

'Mother wants to see you about that today, some time. I think she's rather dreading it.'

'Dreading giving me the sack?' Margot forced a laugh. 'I knew I wasn't staying with you for ever when I was taken on. I needed you at that time, George, with all your cussedness and determination to fight me tooth and nail. I was going through a bad patch, too.'

'And is it better, now?'

'*That's* better, yes.'

'There wouldn't be another one starting, would there?'

'Oh, George!'

'Because all the while I've been yammering on you haven't been listening half the time. I've become very observant of others lately, you know, since I came to my senses again. I'd say at a guess, taking your age and looks into account, that it's some guy.'

Margot blushed. 'George, shut up! You're ready, so off you go and stop poking and prying. I'll tidy up in here.'

As she busied herself last night seemed like a bad dream. Maxine had been very nice and friendly, and the meal she had prepared excellent, but the revelations she had made about Guy's past affairs, and possibly a present one, had shaken Margot's faith in human nature and made her wonder if anyone was ever again to be trusted. Mike had charmed her, and then gone off and married another. Guy's charm had appeared more mature, and herself more deeply involved.

'When I see him this evening, I'm sure he'll explain,' she told herself, as she looked the room and bathroom over and found nothing else needed doing. 'Now I'd better go and see Mrs Whitham and discuss the future. I don't want her to think I'm a hanger-on.'

Emily had a shaded balcony attached to her bedroom, and it was here she usually breakfasted, for the view over the sea was magnificent. Margot, on hearing that her employer was awake, knocked and announced herself as she had often done.

'Oh, Nurse Walsh!' Emily knocked over her coffee-cup and Margot could see that she really was nervous. 'Look at me! I'm so clumsy of a morning. *Do* ring for more coffee, my dear, and include yourself.'

Margot came back from the intercom saying, 'I really

thought we ought to talk about the future. George won't need me much longer.'

Emily immediately relaxed and looked towards the swimming pool, where all her three children were at present sporting.

'It must be great minds thinking alike, I guess,' she smiled, 'but I was thinking the same thing. You need someone sicker than George, really, to keep in practice, don't you? Not that we really want to lose you. John was saying why don't we take you back to England with us and give you a holiday? It would be our way of saying thank you for all you've done.'

'That's very kind of you,' said Margot, as Maria arrived with a tray of fresh coffee and milk. 'But I don't think I should take holidays in excess. It's almost a holiday here now, for me. I'm not really earning my keep.'

'Oh, rubbish!' Mrs Whitham poured the coffee, one cup milky and her own black. 'We're planning to go back home in four weeks' time and you are to stay here until then, as a house-guest, almost. Let's see what George can do and you step in if he gets in trouble. O.K.? If you won't accompany us back to England then I suggest we give you three months' salary in lieu.'

'That's far too generous,' Margot objected. 'I'll take this as a month's notice and study the papers for jobs. You mustn't spoil me.'

'Well, that's rich! Who's spoiling whom? You're getting that cheque in your bank whether you like it or not. So let's enjoy our coffee and watch the kids, eh?'

Another 'kid' had appeared. Ricci was strutting up and down the side of the pool wearing red trunks.

'What do you think of the Italian boy?' asked Emily.

'He seems all right, but I think he should be kept in his place,' said Margot. 'It's none of my business, but he appears to have given himself the run of the Villa Romana.'

The older woman frowned. 'Yes, he's a bit smooth for my liking. I suppose he's a bit lonely, too. So long as it's George and not Tessa he's after.'

Not being too sure on this point herself, Margot drained her coffee-cup and said, 'I'll just go down there and join them and hear what they're planning. If you'll excuse me——?'

'Surely, Nurse Walsh. And—and thanks for being so understanding.'

'Rubbish! Thank *you* for my lovely job.'

She hurried down to the swimming-pool where Tessa was donning her robe and talking to Ricci. George was doing his strong overarm up and down the length of the bath.

'Your mother would like to see you, Tessa,' Margot said pointedly.

'But Mother's not up yet.'

'Oh yes, she is. I've just had coffee with her on her balcony.'

'Oh. O.K., then. See you, Ricci.'

'We have just been planning the most fantastic picnic,' Ricci said, with his usual charm. 'You too, dear Margot, must come.'

'Oh, thanks,' she said. 'Where and when is this picnic?'

'On Sunday, when I have day off. I have chance to borrow minibus from a friend and we get George in the back with his chair, then with your good self, Tessa, Van and little Sophia, we go to a sandy bay I know where we can all swim. It will do George so much good. Tessa has said she will provide the picnic. You agree?'

'I think we must ask Mr and Mrs Whitham before we make such plans. If they agree, certainly I'll come. Can you drive a minibus?'

'Well, perhaps it would be better to take the driver with us. I have only driven a car. If you would be happier ...?'

'Is he willing?'

'For a small fee I think he would be willing,' Ricci grinned. 'I must go now. I have a party of senior citizens coming. 'Bye, George! 'Bye, Van!'

George was lifted from the water by Enrico and wrapped in a warm towelling robe in his chair.

'I'm getting good,' he complimented himself. 'I must've swum half a mile.'

'You *are* getting good,' Margot replied. 'What's this about a picnic on Sunday?'

'It could be fun, don't you think? We have talked about it before.'

'Oh, yes, it *could* be fun. But I always thought you were going to take your first swim in the sea from the villa's private beach, which is just below the house?'

'Ricci says I'll never make it. There's a steep descent from a door in the wall and the door's sealed up. He went to see why and says there's been a rock slide, so there's no path for the first six feet and as the cove's land-locked, I wouldn't be able to get there, huh? He knows a beach which is accessible, even to me, so why all the argument?'

'I'm not arguing.' Margot smiled to show she shared his youthful enthusiasm. All the young folk would be together and she would be in charge, so what harm could come of it? And she was quite prepared to pay the driver his 'small fee' for the peace of mind she could enjoy with an expert at the wheel of the minibus. If the Whitham parents agreed to the outing, or even wanted to join in themselves, then she would be happy to go along.

She slept heavily after lunch and awoke with a start, reminding herself that she had an Italian lesson in less than an hour, and that Guy had said he would meet her afterwards with Teresa, the dog, in tow. They were to go for a walk. All would be explained, she felt suddenly sure, and all would quickly come right between them. Guy just couldn't be capable of playing fast and loose with her emotions. Maxine didn't know the real Guy, twin though she might be, as no sister can ever really know her brother the way other women do.

She showered, dressed, and drank the tea Lucia brought for her, and then told George where she was going.

'Oh, O.K. This came for you.' He passed her a hand-written envelope. 'Lucia said you were way, way gone, so I told her not to wake you. I hope it's nothing important.'

'No. No, it isn't,' said Margot, who had recognised Guy's writing on the envelope.

She opened it in the hall and read its contents disbelievingly.

'Am unavoidably tied up'—he had written—'will be in touch when possible.' There was not even a signature.

Anybody in the villa could have read the message and been little the wiser. Maybe that was what he had thought, that if somebody else opened the note 'by mistake', then not a great deal of information was offered for the trespasser's delectation.

A slow anger burnt into Margot.

'How dare he?' she blazed silently. 'How dare he think he can pick me up and drop me as if I *didn't matter*!'

She was almost over-attentive during her lesson, and yet learnt little, and the strain of trying to concentrate on past participles made her voice uncertain.

'Are you getting a cold, Miss Walsh?' asked Miss MacDougal. 'Possibly you are foolish enough not to wear a vest at all times. Sophia has to be watched or she'll be going back home with pneumonia. I think that will be all for this time. Next week we'll do the shopping in Rome exercise, without books. I'll be the Signora and you'll be Lisa. *Arrivederci!*'

'Psst!' came from the rose-hedge as Margot closed the gate of the Villa Montefiore behind her.

'Sophia? What——?'

'Ssh! I don't want my godmother to hear. May we walk a little way together?'

'Certainly. I'm not doing anything else,' Margot said rather wryly. 'What's the matter? You have a cold, haven't you?'

'No.' Sophia shook her head. 'Though that's what *she* thinks. Always on about vests and things. I—I think I'm broken-hearted and I don't know what to do about it. Actually I thought I wanted to die. But when I considered the ways—well, I changed my mind. And in any case, I don't want to upset my godmother.'

'Who's the young man?' Margot asked, though she already felt she knew.

'It's Ricci. Ricci Lamati. Don't you think he's wonderful? So good-looking and polite and—and—you know ...?'

'No, I don't know. What else is he?'

'Well, he's very attractive. He makes me feel like a mature woman. When he held me in his arms I sort of—melted. I never wanted to leave him.'

'Sophia, tell me honestly, as a friend. What did Ricci do to you?'

'Oh!' Sophia blushed scarlet. 'Oh, not *that*! Not all the way. I asked Ricci if he wanted to marry me and he said maybe—when I came back next year. I was happy with that. But then he changed. He began sending me away. He said he was visiting the Villa Romana to be with George, but he's got his eye on Tessa, hasn't he? I know it's another woman. When you love somebody you *know* these things instinctively. Oh, Nurse Walsh, I'm so unhappy!'

Margot gathered the girl to her and led her off up a little path off the road. There was a grassy hummock and they sat down with the shadows deepening all about them and the sun now just a remembered radiance in the western sky.

'Now listen to me and take heed, Sophia, please. You're much, much too young to be seriously in love with anybody. I know you might not believe me, but it's true. I was in love with my geometry master when I was sixteen, and the very next year with a man whose name I never knew, who just drove past my house in an E-type Jaguar. I grew out of both of these infatuations, which is what they really were.' Margot looked grave. 'Now Ricci has no right to touch you, or play on your emotions, because they have obviously leapt ahead of your reasoning power temporarily. Believe me, Sophia, all this is really very temporary. I could almost guarantee that by next year you'll have forgotten Ricci Lamati. He's doing a lot of good for George, but don't worry about competition from Tessa. She's a young lady with her head screwed on very firmly and George has his eye on Ricci in that direction, too. I think Ricci is an opportunist, and is ingratiating himself with the Whitham family at present. You've heard about the picnic planned for Sunday?'

'No!'

'Oh, yes. You're invited, too. We're all going in a mini-bus to some beach, so try not to be too serious about Ricci and just enjoy yourself, eh? *I'll* be there and you can bet Ricci's not going to do any kissing and cuddling with anybody under *my* eagle eye.'

Sophia chuckled softly and then sighed.

'Physical love isn't all that important,' Margot went on, and wondered how she could say such things, who had truly lost her own head in the company of a man only two days ago. 'It's liking each other that's really vital. When you like somebody you trust them. Passion is blind and can cause a lot of hurt. Now look on this summer visit as an experience, and profit from it.'

'I wish I was as wise as you are, Nurse Walsh.'

'Oh, come on! I've been stupid in my time, too, and believed people meant things when they didn't. Now I'm going to see you back to your house, just in case you think you might sneak off looking for romance. Do you feel better?'

'Oh, much. A fellow-feeling makes us wondrous kind

—somebody once wrote that in my diary. I feel that you, too, have suffered and know the score. It's been good talking things over with another woman.'

'Goodnight, then,' Margot held open the gate of the Villa Montefiore. 'Somebody will tell you about the picnic. So if I don't see you before——'

'I'll look forward to it. Goodnight, Nurse Walsh.'

The next day hope sprang up that Guy would appear again.

'He said he would be in touch when possible,' Margot told herself. 'Nothing has happened, really, to change things. I got gossiping with Maxine, who hadn't a clue how things really are between Guy and me, and so she told me things she maybe shouldn't, and implied he was off after a woman she obviously loathed. I should have known better than to doubt him, because I *do* know how things are between us. Has he said he doesn't care about me? No, only that he's unavoidably held up with something or somebody. He'll call, or ring, or——'

Maxine rang. She sounded cheerful.

'I say, Margot, are you free? Can you come over for tea and cucumber sandwiches? I have the most astounding news for you.'

'Yes, I'll be over, Maxine. Is—is Guy there?'

'No. We can have another girl-to-girl chat.'

Margot's heart had sunk again. She told Mrs Whitham whither she was bound and set off in the hot sunlight of afternoon for the Villa Fiorita. She noticed it particularly on this occasion, as though storing it in her remembrance, a small, open-fronted villa drenched in maroon and cream bougainvillaea, and sinking back into its garden where there were shady old trees; a lemon, with pale globes of fruit among its dark leaves, a spreading walnut and several old olives. At the back was a vine-covered patio, and here Maxine had laid out the tea things.

'I don't know where to begin,' she said girlishly, holding out a plate of wafer-thin sandwiches and pouring pale China tea into eggshell-thin cups. 'The other night Paolo almost eloped with me. You saw us, I think? He just drove on and on saying that unless I named the date he wouldn't stop the car and we might finish up in the Arctic. I said that if Guy came home and I was missing he might be worried and he said "Damn Guy!" or something like that, and what about *him*? He's sweet. You'd like him,' she added inconsequently.

'Well, I said I'd have to break it to Guy very gently, as we were so close and I'd promised to go to Venezuela with him, and everything, so on the understanding that I broached my news, Paolo took me home at two a.m., and we needn't have worried because Guy didn't come back until four. He was tired when he had to get up and a bit cross, so I snapped back at him and told him I was going to marry Paolo, and he asked Paolo who, and did I know what I was doing? Just then Paolo arrived and I could see they approved one another on sight. Guy said we'd talk later as he had to go and take morning clinic. I called after him what about Venezuela? And he said oh, forget that. No problem. He called in briefly in the afternoon and said he was happy for me. I told him that I was very much in love and he said he was glad. Am I making sense?

'I asked him how about joining Paolo and me for

dinner, somewhere, but he said sorry, he had to go to Siena. I said, "To see Yvonne, I suppose?" That's Yvonne Mountstewart—I told you about her, didn't I? He said if I was intending to be happy ever after I had better forget old bitterness, and that he intended seeing exactly whom he chose, when he chose, without asking my permission. "You have fallen in love with your Paolo," he said, "and I'm very happy for you. I may even now consider marriage myself, in due course, but I've got myself involved in something rather unfortunate, which I feel I must see through decently to the end. I'm not confiding further in you," he said, "because you're so wrapped up in your own affairs you'd probably get the wrong end of the stick. Try to keep out of mischief," and off he went. He—he left a letter for you. I'll get it.'

Maxine returned with a plain envelope and handed it over.

'Had you a date with Guy or something?' she asked with interest. 'Because while he was shaving I heard him saying, "How am I going to explain to Margot? How could I have known this was going to happen?" I asked, "What was that, Guy?" as though I hadn't heard, and he said, "Oh, nothing. I'm just thinking aloud." Then he scribbled that letter.'

'No, we had no definite plans for anything,' Margot said, deliberately putting the unopened envelope into her bag. 'I would love another cup of tea, Maxine, please.'

How she hung on without opening the letter until she was back at the Villa Romana, and safely in her room for the night, she would never know. She got through dinner appearing her usual self, and all the time wondering what Guy had to say to her this time, and when she at last ripped open the envelope she felt almost afraid to read.

'My dear Margot.' Well, that was better than his last effort!

'I fear you must wonder at my apparent neglect. Well, you of all people will understand that something very important has cropped up. I can only explain when I see you, and I don't really know when that will be. Maxine has some terrific news of her own that she will no doubt be sharing with you. I feel I should warn you that our past relationship is cancelled out entirely. This requires further clarification, I know. Please be patient with

Yours,

Guy.'

Margot sat on the edge of her bed feeling absolutely benumbed. She read the letter again and in every word there now appeared to be rejection. 'Our past relationship is cancelled out entirely' ... 'This requires further clarification' ... but did it? He obviously regretted their past together and was trying to prepare her for the bitter truth. She remembered Maxine rambling on, saying something about Guy being involved in something unfortunate, which he felt bound to see through, in all decency, to the end. Well, *she* must be the unfortunate involvement, and when she remembered, it was she who had been the more eager partner in their relationship. She had been the one who was eager for a marriage between them. She felt humiliated and unhappy. She wanted to write something in haste, her pen tipped in bitterness, like, 'Don't worry about me! You owe me nothing. Explanations are quite unnecessary. Just consider our relationship automatically cancelled.' But fortunately she didn't write a word, though she sat with pen poised over paper for more than an hour before she finally slipped into bed knowing full well that sleep would be elusive and the hours of the night slow to pass on heavy, leaden feet.

CHAPTER EIGHT

THERE was a paper lying on the breakfast bar when Margot approached, heavy-eyed, next morning. It was a copy of *The Times* Mr Whitham had thoughtfully left for her, because she had expressed a wish to see about a new job and *The Times* was as good a medium as any. She opened it at random and seeing a headline, 'Why are some people born to be losers?' closed the paper hurriedly. She was surely one of the world's losers, and didn't want to wallow with someone else's troubles unless she could actually help.

She took a cup of coffee and the paper and looked resolutely at the 'Appointments Vacant' columns. So many people wanted secretaries that she decided she had chosen the wrong profession. She imagined herself as a secretary, svelte and accomplished and living in London, of course, in a flat shared by one other girl, perhaps. Her boss would treasure her and maybe some of his rivals would woo her, maybe over the phone. 'Oh, Miss Walsh, if you do ever think of leaving old Gimble there's always a job for you here. And of course, a raise in salary. Name

your own figure ...' Regular hours and home to the flat;
an immaculate kitchen with pot plants in the window
and the bathroom always tidy. She wouldn't have her
flatmate using it as a laundry with strings tied across.
There would be boy-friends, of course. Her flatmate's
would sometimes stay overnight—well, one had to be
broad-minded about these things—but hers——!

Here the day-dream came to a full stop. She just
couldn't imagine any Tom, Dick or Harry beside her in
her immaculate bed, not unless that special ring was on
her finger. Maybe this was what was wrong with her, that
she had failed to make the jump in moral standards so
many of her contemporaries took in their stride. Maybe
she had disappointed Guy in that respect?

Speculation was getting her nowhere and she returned
to the 'Appointments Vacant'. There were two possi-
bilities in her field:

*Wanted: trained nurse to live in and look after elderly
invalid. Own room. T.V. Generous off-duty.*
and the other, which had more appeal: *Wanted: young
nurse to travel to Kenya with family. Five-year-old blue-
baby girl awaiting operation.*

'Oh, poor little kiddy!' Margot's generous heart went
out to the small invalid, who she knew would be only as
big as a normal two-and-a-half-year-old child. 'I think
I'll write in about that.' But she discovered the paper was
already two days old and decided that people would
already have phoned in. Only a London phone number
was given.

She pondered for a while. 'My best plan is to put an
advertisement in the *Nursing Mirror*, and use the Villa
Romana as an address. I still have a month. That way

I may get a choice of jobs, or I'll just have to go back into hospital and work.'

A feeling of excitement spread through the Villa Romana all day on Saturday. Tessa went off with Giovanna to the local market to help buy food she wanted for the morrow's picnic. She returned and said, blithely, that Giovanna had almost fainted at the money she had spent. The woman, with the help of the girls Lucia and Maria, was now boiling crabs and a lobster, and they were only for starters.

'It sounds more like a feast than a picnic,' Margot opined. 'Any food tastes good in the open air, Tessa.'

'Oh, go on, Nurse Walsh! Eat, drink and be merry—you know the rest. We're going to have a fabulous picnic that nobody's going to forget.'

Margot had dropped a hint that young Sophia was feeling a little low and lonely, and so Tessa had invited her over. They went off with pencils and notebooks to make out lists of everything they would need on the picnic, and because it was Saturday, and there were plenty of visitors to the ruins, there was no Ricci to distract the girls, and George and Van had their own ways of entertaining themselves.

Margot composed her advertisement and whenever her thoughts threatened to depress her she turned quickly to reading, and so the day passed, for her, as slowly as the previous night had done. There was a sudden thunderstorm in the evening and out of it, his hair plastered to his head, and looking somehow more like a demon from the elements of darkness than the demi-god of Margot's first impressions, stepped Ricci, into the family's midst.

'So sorry! So sorry!' he kept saying, as he was led off

to dry himself. It was the cocktail hour and when he came back Emily automatically offered the Italian a drink.

'Oh, no, thank you so much.'

'We must lend you one of George's shirts.'

'No, no. I now go to my digs, where I change.' He seemed nervous, Margot fancied, or it may just have been that he felt a little foolish standing there soaked to the skin. 'I just wanted to know that tomorrow is O.K. My friend with the minibus comes at nine o'clock.'

'Sure, everything's O.K.,' George assured him. 'My mother just wanted to be sure that the driver has a licence. She has her own reasons for asking.'

'Rodolfo is qualified driver. He drive children to school when not holidays.'

'Then sure it's O.K., Ricci. We'll be ready by nine, as arranged. Now you either change into some of my clothes or go home.'

'I must go.' Ricci laughed and looked round the group. 'You *are* coming, Margot?'

'Yes, I had planned to. I can drop out if there isn't room, or something ...?'

'Oh, no, I want you should come. Then that is fine. Sorry I interrupt.'

'Not at all. The storm seems to be over now. See Mr Lamati out, Lucia.' Emily pondered over her glass of Cinzano. 'A funny boy, that. I always get the feeling he's not quite real. He could be a character in the book one's reading and when you finish it he's gone.'

'Now that's woman talk!' said her husband, drawing comfortably on his pipe, his drink to hand. 'Making romance where none exists, as usual. He's a poor boy with a bit of education and a few—to him—rich friends whom he intends to exploit to the full while he can. He'll already have worked out his commission from the bus-owner in advance. He's as real as you and me, Emmie, and I don't mind him taking his cut out of me so long as all the kids have fun, and Nurse Walsh sees to it they don't have too much. I'm glad you're going along, my dear'—he looked directly at Margot—'I was a bit worried for a moment there, when I thought he was giving you a let-out.'

'You know what you're managing to do, Mother—Dad?' George asked. 'You're making Ricci appear sinister. He's just a kid. Now everybody be quiet and let's look forward to our trip. I know I am!'

The Sunday morning, after the thunderstorm, was not only extremely hot but humid. Margot found herself rising from a perspiration-soaked bed only to shower and then immediately start to perspire again. She found George also feeling the heat as she helped him to dress in light clothes for the picnic.

'We should all enjoy a swim in the sea today,' she decided, as she helped him into his lightweight folding chair, instead of the one which could be electrically motivated if he required to travel long distances around the villa and its grounds.

In the courtyard in front of the villa stood a white-painted minibus, with both back doors thrown wide. There was a great deal of pandemonium as Tessa and Sophia, sometimes helped, and often hindered, by young Van, stored all the gear. Picnic hampers went in, and bundles of linen and towels and swimming things. Even a red-and-white striped circular tent went in, which Tessa had thought of in case there was nowhere private for the girls to change.

Lucia came out staggering under a refrigerated container for drinks and butter, et cetera.

'Now have we got salt and pepper and a tin opener?' Tessa asked, reading from the list in her hand.

'Yes,' Sophia confirmed. 'I packed them into the first basket and marked it with a number.'

'Then that's about it,' Tessa decided. 'We'd better get up front and leave the rear for George and his chair. Where's Ricci?' she suddenly asked, in puzzlement. 'Anybody seen him?'

She asked the bus-driver in Italian, who answered at great length.

'He wants to be picked up in the village. He had something to do. Come on, everybody! Van! You are *not* taking Herbert.'

Herbert was Van's pet snake. It even slept—if snakes do—in his room.

'Oh, but I am. I promised him.'

'Mother!' Emily had arrived in a housecoat with her husband behind her, smoking his first pipe of the day. 'Tell Van he can't take Herbert. He gives some of us the creepies.'

'Van,' said John Whitham solemnly, 'in addition to what your sister says I don't think Herbert will like salt water, and he's going to need shade from the sun. Why not leave him at home and I'll look after him? You can't be nursemaid to a snake all day.'

'O.K., then,' said Van, handing over a cardboard box

into his father's care. 'Find him a couple of frogs. This is one of his eating days.'

Enrinco and Salvatore lifted George into the rear of the minibus and Margot turned for a moment and saw Guy in the wide-open gateway. He was wearing the faded old red-checked shirt of their first meeting and blue denims.

'Hello!' he greeted. 'What's going on here?'

'Good morning, Doctor Massey. We're going on a picnic.'

She turned away deliberately to do something for George, but he was by her side.

'You got my letters?'

'Oh, yes,' she said flatly, 'I got your letters.'

She felt like the lost little girl of fairy tale whose heart had been turned to ice under a wicked spell. She couldn't feel anything of an emotional nature.

'Then when *can* I see you?' he asked, and at her blank look, 'so that we can have our talk?'

'I really don't know what there can be to say. You owe no duty to me. Now, if you'll excuse me——?'

All in a moment his hand had reached out and whirled her round to face him. She almost expected him to strike her, such fire came from his blue eyes.

'Well, enjoy your picnic,' he said slowly, at length. 'I mustn't hold up the expedition.'

Margot climbed into the back beside George and the back doors were shut and locked. The youngsters in the front cheered as the engine roared into life.

'What's up with you, Nurse?' George asked in her ear above the racket. 'You just gave a perfectly nice guy the frozen mitt.'

'What business is it of yours, George, what I do?'

'Because you didn't enjoy it, and he didn't either.' George observed. 'And it concerns me because you're going to be in a grim mood all day and take it out on me.'

She looked at him unhappily.

'No, O.K. You never take things out on me. What gives between you and Doctor Massey? He's a great guy.'

'Many people think so. Lots of other women.'

'Oh, so it's hell hath no fury, is it? Well——'

'Now listen, George, either you shut up or I get out,' Margot said. 'This one day I want to forget all about Doctor Massey.'

'O.K., O.K., so I'll say no more on the subject. Here's Ricci! Hi there!'

'Hello, everybody! Very hot, isn't it?'

Ricci looked pale and shadows were dark under his eyes.

'Aren't you well, Ricci?' Margot asked, as the Italian lit up a cigarette and puffed deeply.

'I didn't sleep well. A toothache, I fear. Tomorrow I must go to dentist.'

'Doctor Agostini would have given you an injection, I'm sure,' said Margot.

'Oh, it is much better now. You know how things hurt in the night which seem so much better in the morning?' He shouted instructions to the driver, who replied with a grunt. The bus travelled inland, away from the wide coastal road, and the drive was quite picturesque. Only when they met the odd car, or farm wagon, on narrow bends was there a sudden braking, and breaths held while passage was slowly negotiated.

Margot was glad Ricci was not doing the driving. She glanced at him occasionally, but he spent his time looking out of the window and exchanging an occasional remark with the driver.

After an hour they dipped towards the coast again, which hereabouts was very rugged. Now Ricci really took charge. He guided the driver under cliff overhangs and round sharp bends until there was a parking place, and there the bus was stopped.

'Here we get out,' he announced, 'and take everything down to the beach.'

'What beach?' asked Tessa.

'You will see,' Ricci smiled at last.

'What about George?' Margot asked.

'No trouble. We get him down *pronto*.'

He and the driver lifted George in his chair to the ground, and then disappeared with him into some gorse bushes. Margot followed, surprised to see a sharp incline had been cut into the cliff and George was being wheeled down it with Ricci in front and the driver behind. They arrived in a sandy cove which was a complete surprise, as it could not be seen from the road because the cliff overhung it. The sand was almost white and the sea lapped on to it with a faint and pleasant swishing sound.

The youngsters came running down to see, whooped with joy and then willingly ran up and down the path emptying the bus of their belongings.

'Isn't this gorgeous?' Tessa asked as she helped to erect the tent. 'Good for Ricci, huh?'

'Yes, good for Ricci,' Margot agreed. 'I forgot to put George's swimming trunks on underneath. May we use the tent first?'

'Of course, Nurse Walsh. Go ahead!'

George was soon wearing only red swimming trunks and was out of his chair and stretched out on a towel. He covered himself with sun-oil while Margot changed. The two younger girls were already in the shallows, splashing each other. Van was digging out small crabs and watching them scuttle back into the sand again.

'Well, George, ready for your dip in the sea?' asked Margot as she emerged in her own swimming costume, a black and white one on this occasion.

'Say, Nurse, you look fantastic, you know that? You have some figure!'

'Well, thank you, kind sir. Ricci! I'll need you to help.'

Ricci was for some reason half way up the cliff and looking at the view beyond the cove. He came running, however, and summoned the bus-driver, who was settling down to a cigarette in the shade. They made a 'chair' for George and then, because the driver was not undressed, Ricci took the invalid on his shoulders with utter ease and did not let him go until the water was deep enough to support George's weight.

'You're surprisingly strong, Ricci,' Margot said in grudging admiration.

'Oh, yes.' Ricci was not modest. 'I am, as you say, a man of many parts.'

They were soon all swimming, apart from Van, who was now poking about in holes in the cliff, but he was not a boy who got into mischief and Margot did not feel she had to watch out for him. He was quite capable of studying a spider or a lizard for hours, in a natural world of his own. Obviously Van was cut out to be a zoologist or a vet.

Margot was the first to leave the water and used the tent before the rush started to dry herself and dress. She emerged combing her hair and looking fondly at the youngsters still in the water, which was particularly warm on this day and so she had no fears for anyone taking a chill. Ricci and George were having a kind of wrestling match, which involved pushing each other under the water and then changing position. Knowing George's lung capacity Margot didn't fret for him when it was his turn to go under. She settled down on a towel as they broke apart and began to swim. To the sound of youthful shrieking and laughter and George's peculiar dark-brown guffaw, she looked up at the sky beyond the overhang and allowed her mind to wander.

She had given herself the summer to get over Mike's defection, which was why she had taken this job. How long ago it all seemed now; her mother's death and the funeral, the hiatus her mind became while she was selling the house, and then the news of Mike's engagement and the ending of another chapter. Endings—endings—and then a new beginning as Guy's shabbily-dressed but haughty figure had loomed in her view on that first, never-to-be-forgotten occasion when she had, at her most high and mighty, ordered him off the premises of the Villa Romana, herself dripping and angry and determined to spite somebody.

The weeks after that had passed excitingly, for there had not only been a beginning but a splendid development as, in music, the intricacy of a fugue follows the melody of the prelude. It had appeared that they were crashing towards some grand finale, she and Guy. She didn't quite know what would happen now. Love suspended grows cool—one cannot prolong ecstasy indefinitely—and Guy's unreasonable behaviour in dashing off to see another woman at such a time, a woman who his sister said had been one of his 'amours', insulted the whole concept of love. Love left waiting ceases to be emotion and becomes bitter juices souring the system. It asks questions of itself and, receiving no answers, loses its confidence. The lover, feeling rejected, mounts such defences that she is safe as a crustacean in its shell from further assault, and no one can suspect the softness still within. This is nature's way of creating defence mechanisms, and Margot had subconsciously developed hers.

'But why did he come this morning, unannounced?' she now asked herself. 'And what did he want to talk about? If it was to get rid of me I think I've safely accomplished that. I've saved my pride, at least, as I saved it with Mike. I think I may be intended to lead a very proud life but a very lonely one.'

She sat up suddenly as Tessa's voice intruded with a note of urgency.

'Nurse Walsh! Nurse Walsh! George is swimming out to sea and he won't stop!'

Margot sat up and saw a figure striking out strongly, over-arm, and rapidly disappearing from view.

'George!' she joined in the shouting, but a swimmer in the water is partly deafened by his efforts and it was doubtful that George could hear anything.

Margot felt the panic she had experienced when George had apparently lain prone on the bottom of the swimming pool at the Villa. She turned to Ricci and said more sharply than she intended, 'Well? This was all *your* idea. Aren't you going to do anything?'

For a moment his eyes were darkly resentful as he looked at her and then, without a word, he waded into the water and struck out.

'It's not Ricci's fault,' Tessa said uncomfortably.

'I'm sorry. He's the only one capable of swimming out so far, though, isn't he? I'd go myself if I was any good.'

It seemed ages before the two heads, the one blond and the other carrot-topped, bobbed together in the distance and then George seemed to be arguing and made rude gestures in the direction of the watchers on the beach, including an unmistakable thumb to nose.

'Oh, he's O.K.,' Tessa laughed. The two swimmers were now swimming back towards the cove. 'Golly, but I'm hungry! Are you, Sophia?'

'Yes, I could eat a horse.'

'Oh, you don't have to do that. We've got fresh crab and Parma ham. Let's change before George needs the tent.'

'What was all the hoo-ha, for Pete's sake?' George asked, as he emerged on Ricci's shoulders out of the water. 'I was enjoying myself, practising for the Paraplegic Olympics maybe.'

'If that's your ambition, I'm sure there are proper places to train with expert supervisors,' Margot replied. 'You had only to get an attack of cramp, and then where would you be? Thanks, Ricci,' she said awkwardly, realising that she always had a tendency to dislike him without a logical reason. 'You must be tired. Put him down on the towel, please.'

'O.K., George?' Ricci asked, without responding to her.

Both girls had changed into dry bikinis—they were

expecting to swim again after lunch had been digested—but Margot decided George had done enough and helped him to dress.

'You can lie down after lunch and have a nap,' she told him.

The alfresco meal was set out appetisingly on a blue-chequered cloth. Giovanna had baked the rolls and pastries. The white crab-meat was laid out in a huge dish of salad and the Parma ham was in rolls filled with olives and chives. Everyone set to with great gusto until it was realised Van wasn't with them.

'I'll get him,' volunteered Tessa, who had been the last to see him, and ran off.

'What about the driver, Ricci?' asked Margot.

'Oh,' he answered coolly, 'he eats his own food. He is working-class man and prefers to eat alone.'

Margot glanced at the man, who was sitting facing the cliff so that he had his back to the party. He appeared to be biting at a whole loaf of bread, but she knew that it would be a typical local sandwich, the bread split in half, unbuttered, for butter was considered a needless extravagance, and filled with either ripe local cheese or salami. Tessa and Van joined the group, she saying sharply, 'He was making friends with an eel. Why do his friends always have to be slimy?'

The main course was followed by Giovanna's special dessert, a pastry tart filled with raisins, chopped nuts and marzipan. Not everybody got as far as the fresh fruit; peaches, bananas, grapes and fat, yellow pears. Most of the youngsters had drunk their fill of Coca-cola and bottled citron, and only George joined Margot in a desire for coffee from a flask. First one and then another curled up for the traditional siesta, and as she had had no part in the laying out of the feast Margot undertook to clear most of the remains away. Van insisted on helping her.

'Don't you want a nap?' Margot asked.

'No,' said Van. 'I'm never tired in the daytime. Life's too interesting to lose whole hours at a time. What shall I do with the empty cans?'

'I think they'll be buried later, but I don't think we should make a clatter now, do you? Just fancy, this gorgeous beach, and we have it all to ourselves! There isn't another soul for miles.'

'Oh, but there is—are,' Van corrected. 'When I was up the cliff there, I saw three other guys.'

'What were they doing? Fishing or something?'

'No, they were just sitting and talking quietly, and smoking. They may have been gambling. I think they had a pack of cards.'

Margot looked at the buttress of rocks which sealed them inside the cove, and wondered now what lay beyond.

'What an odd place to come to gamble,' she commented, folding up the cloth. 'They do it in every bar and *trattoria*, and we *are* rather a long way from the towns.'

'Maybe they're murderers on the run,' Van said simply and dramatically. 'I didn't speak to them and they didn't see me, because you never know.'

'Van!' said Margot, with a laugh which came too quickly to be convincing. 'What an imagination you've got! Now don't go off and find any more unsavoury characters, because I'm going to close my eyes for just five minutes, and I don't want to open them and find you missing. Try having just a little nap. Out of a whole lifetime I'm sure you won't miss too much action in fifteen minutes or so.'

Margot opened her eyes thankfully, escaping from some unremembered doom locked away in her subconscious mind. Now she regretted having fallen asleep and looked around her sharply, automatically accounting for the members of the party. They still slept; even Van was out for the count, pillowing his head on one arm as he lay on his stomach. The bus-driver was grunting in his sleep. Margot looked across at Ricci, who now regarded her with an unwinking, brown-eyed stare.

'So somebody else is awake,' she whispered with a smile.

'I do not sleep all the time. I just lie here and think.'

'Oh? What do you think about, Ricci?'

'That would be telling. Thoughts are private things.'

'I'm sorry,' she said, 'I didn't mean to pry.'

'All the time you don't mean, Margot, but you do just the same.'

'I don't understand you, Ricci.'

'I think you understand me well. When I offer to be your friend, to talk English with you, you say yes with your mouth but no with your eyes. I am George's friend very quickly, but you disapprove; I know the way you look at me. You send Tessa away from me when we are just talking, and I know what you are thinking and I hate you for it. You think I would hurt young girls? *Little* girls? I think of them like my own sisters. I would kill anybody who hurt them. You do not want me for yourself, but you do not want anybody else to have me.

I tell you I have had lovers, many, many lovers; I am a man, not a little boy. But always I love with women, *not* children, even when they are foolish and romantic like little Sophia, there.

'I wanted to love *you*, Margot,' he said bitterly, 'I dreamed often about it. But always you are cold towards me. I think, perhaps you find out that I tell lies about myself, that I am really a poor boy, a boy from the streets who—who denies his own mother.'

He paused to weep into his hands, as easily emotional as any Latin. Margot crept towards him and put out a comforting hand. 'No, don't touch me! I am not fit to be touched when I will not admit I am ashamed of my own mother. Always we have been poor, my father died in a mining accident when I was ten. I am not a medical student; I worked in a chemist's shop before I got this job; I was sacked because the chemist's wife wanted me to love her. You are shocked? I can see in your eyes. Always I am this way with women, until you.

'What is wrong with me that you pull away when I am near you, Margot?' he demanded. 'Am I not handsome or how you call it? Is my body not good? You send me into the sea to save George like I am a servant. You think I let my friend drown before my eyes? I do not need sending from you.'

She flushed. 'Well, I'm sorry, Ricci, if I've offended you. I didn't mean——'

'You see? Again you didn't mean, but you do it.'

'Well, what can I say? I don't feel romantically about you, but that doesn't mean you're not good-looking or attractive. I'm not looking for that kind of relationship with you, that's all.'

'That is good, because now is too late.'

'Oh? Well, nobody got hurt, then.'

'*I* got hurt. But doesn't matter.'

'Of course it matters. But if you are attractive to so many women you won't miss one who didn't—er—love you for long.'

'No. You are so right. Now I don't love you any more.'

Margot could think of nothing to say to that but 'Good!'

Looking away, she saw George's interested and amused gaze.

'Don't let me intrude on your intriguing conversation,' he said blandly. 'Just carry on as though I wasn't here.'

'Oh, George!'

Ricci rose and walked towards the sea, the muscles rippling under his golden, down-covered skin.

'You could do worse than him,' George opined. 'Good looking, sound in wind and limb and experienced.'

'Oh, George!' she repeated, shortly, 'shut up, do!'

'I didn't know you and he were——'

'Because he and I weren't, if you heard most of the conversation. That's what he was complaining about.'

'What's with you, Nurse? That's the second guy you've rejected today. It's me, isn't it? You're secretly in love with me. Every time you give me an alcohol rub you think how wonderful I am and how cosy we'd be——'

Margot slapped the sand hard with her hand and next minute George gave a cry of genuine, surprised pain. Tessa shot awake asking 'What? What?'

'Oh, George, I'm sorry! Have you some sand in your eye?' Margot felt for a tissue in her bag. 'Here, let me see.'

While Margot dealt with the emergency the other three youngsters ran yelping down to the sea, like healthy young puppies wanting to play after their rest.

'Is that better?' Margot asked softly. 'Oh, George, you asked what was with me today—I don't know, honestly. I'm in a sort of mental and emotional tizzy. Part of it's to do with job-finding, wondering what I'm going to do, and part of it's my personal problem. But I shouldn't take my frustration out on you, of all people.'

'Any time,' George said courteously, trying not to rub his streaming eye. 'Where does Ricci come in?'

'He doesn't. I suppose I did get a sort of "Come hither" from him, but I wasn't interested. He has apparently brooded about it.'

They looked seawards where Van was threatening the two girls with an angry little crab he had discovered. Ricci was some distance out, occasionally doing a backstroke and then floating, his god-like profile turned skywards.

A figure loomed over the watchers on the sand. It was the bus-driver. He spoke to George.

'He says in half an hour we ought to be starting back. He's booked to take a family party to Siena this evening. I'll call the kids.'

George yelled and Margot put oddments she found lying about into the picnic baskets. Ricci was the last to leave the water. In bare feet he climbed the rocky breakwater which sealed the cove in on one side. Margot wandered towards him intending to look at the view beyond.

'Nothing to see there,' he said, quite chummily. 'I am sorry I am such a sourpuss.' He held out his hand, which she could not ignore. She shook it and he then put one arm round her shoulders—'Only friendship, you see? I think the bus-driver wants us to hurry. Already five o'clock, is it? How time hastens!'

Ricci, once dressed, organised everybody else into re-packing the bus. He sent the girls up with the baskets and Van with the tent; everybody then took the wet costumes they had worn wrapped in damp towels to put on the racks in the bus.

'Now we pack George and Nurse Walsh,' Ricci de-cided, nodding to the driver to help. 'You kids stay here and I'll come and help you to tidy up.'

As is always the case, the bus was more untidily packed with the empties than when they had set out with everything full. Margot shoved a bathing bag to safety, which looked as though it might fall on George the moment the bus moved, and then cleared a bit of a seat for herself. She saw the driver come up from below and light a cigarette from the stub of the one in his mouth. He leaned nonchalantly against a smooth boulder and puffed deeply. She watched in a kind of fascination as the smoke seemed to have disappeared into his system, and then it emerged, from his mouth and nose—she even imagined it came from his ears—in the way of the true addict who automatically inhales.

'Poor soul! It's lung cancer for him if he doesn't watch out,' she thought, as a fit of coughing suddenly racked him. She turned away as he hawked and spat, out of a feeling of delicacy.

What happened next she couldn't be quite sure. She saw a figure, which was not the driver's, climb up into the driving seat. It was clad in dark clothes and the thick mop of hair showed it to be a young man. She looked back and the driver was unaccountably lying on the ground, prone, wth an ooze of blood coming from his grizzled skull above his left ear. Two men were bending over him, both with stocking masks over their faces and one brandishing a cosh.

'*Avanti!*' one called, and leapt into the back of the bus with his companion on his tail.

'Hey!' George exclaimed. 'We're being kidnapped!'

Margot opened her mouth to scream only to find a hand clamped over it, and at the same moment the cosh caught George a mighty thwack on the side of his head, which lolled grotesquely. Margot wondered if the assailant had broken his neck. Her eyes were wide and questioning as tape was stuck across her mouth, and then she was roughly dragged to the floor of the bus to be trussed up like a chicken. She wasn't sure, but she fancied that before she had been seized she had seen Ricci's face peering at the scene through the gorse-bushes on the cliff-top. As the bus roared off she thought, 'Well, at least somebody knows. He must have seen something,' and then as she began to feel dizzy she knew what was happening. The fumes from an ether pad were entering her lungs and making her lose consciousness. No matter how she tried to avoid it there was no way she could fight two grown thugs determined to rob her of her senses. She had always wondered what patients felt like under ether, though most of them were injected first with a knock-out drug so that they would not experience the choking sensations of olden days. Now she went through the experience of ringings in her ears, a feeling of a leaden weight on her chest, as though to take another breath was an impossible task, then she entered a dark tunnel and fell deeper and deeper into a well of blackness ...

CHAPTER NINE

MARGOT felt like some disembodied spirit trying to climb out of a grave. It was so dark, with a smell of dried earth about the place. She sat up, after deciding she wasn't yet a spirit, and felt dreadfully nauseated. Of course—she took deep breaths—the ether would account for that. Once she had her stomach under control she was aware of noise, a deep swishing sound which crescended and then receded, and a human groan.

'George!' she called out. 'Is that you?'

'You there, Nurse? Thank God! I thought I'd been buried alive. I've literally got a sore head, after being one for so long.'

'Just a minute, George, I'll find you. Ouch!' She had stumbled the wrong way into what appeared to be a rock ledge. 'Call again, George, to give me direction. My head's not so good, either. Those thugs anaesthetised me after they coshed you. Do you remember?'

'I remember. Hey, they didn't——?' There was an embarrassed silence which spoke volumes, and for the first time she faced the question herself.

'No, I seem to be fine except for a tendency to float off. Ah, there you are.' She had almost fallen over him. 'Where's your chair?' she demanded.

'You don't think they'd bury me in my chair, do you? I seem to be on a sort of mattress. If my head didn't bang so I'd be quite comfortable.'

'I have some aspirins in my bag. Oh, damn!' She never used bad language and George positively jumped. 'They wouldn't have given me my handbag, would they? Not with a few thousand lire in it.' She paused for a moment while a kind of panic washed over her and then she asserted an iron self control. 'Stay where you are, George, I'm going to feel my way around.'

They were in a sort of cell, she decided, as she felt round the walls and ran her fingers over stone ledges. She came to what she thought was a doorway, but it wasn't, it was just that the fresh air came from here and the noise was greater. She had another sudden inspiration and fell to her knees and crawled.

Her disappointment knew no bounds as a faint grey light appeared, only one degree paler than total darkness, and her reaching hands met unrelenting steel bars. She shook these to rid herself of disappointment and aggression and then she crawled back.

'George,' she called, 'I think I know where we are. We're in a secret cave under the old castle. The noise is the sea breaking against the cliffs. I once came here with Ricci, but he did mention he was going to seal up the entrance as it was so dangerous. It's true—it's all sealed up. We're prisoners.'

'Then how come they got us in?'

'I don't know. Maybe there's another way in. These cliffs are riddled with caves. If I'm where I think I am I'll continue all the way round to you. If only I could see! You haven't your illuminated watch on, have you, George?'

'Not to go swimming, Nurse, which was what I set out to do, if you remember? Also, I doubt they'd have left anything on me they could remove.'

'It must be the middle of the night.' There was a sudden clatter. 'Now what have I done?' Margot asked fretfully.

A moment later there was the flicker of a match which she put triumphantly to a large candle. She couldn't help but remember Ricci's store of such things behind the reredos of the old church. She held the candle up to look triumphantly across at George.

'Hello, there! How do I look by candlelight?'

'Wonderful! What else have you got there?'

'Well, it begins to look as though we're expected to be here some time. There are four of these large candles, but we'll ration ourselves anyhow. Also there's a first-aid kit.' She opened the box. 'Oh, good! Some Panadol. They'll have to do for your headache. Also there's bottled mineral water and rations of—let me see—biscuits, cheese, chocolate—— Oh, we won't starve! I see I have a mattress, too. I must have rolled off it while I was so confused. We're quite cosy really, and soon there'll be daylight.'

'Could anybody hear us if we shouted?' enquired George.

'I doubt it. It's very noisy here, and hundreds of seabirds perch on the ledges all about. When I came here I thought one was going to peck out my eyes.'

'You came with Ricci, you say? Why didn't you tell me about it?'

'He asked me not to tell anyone——' she stopped as she anticipated George's next question.

'Do you think Ricci would've had anything to do with this?'

'Oh, George, I don't know. I'm not going to think badly of anybody until I have to. You heard our conversation this afternoon? How he said I was always not meaning to do things, and then doing them? I think you ought to take two tablets and settle down to sleep. I will, too. We can talk in the morning. There! Now, when I get back to my mattress I'm going to blow the candle out. Goodnight, George!'

'Goodnight, Nurse! I couldn't have been kidnapped with anybody I would have preferred to you!'

'You may change your mind when I start on you to-morrow,' she retorted. 'Exercises, massage—we're not going to take this lying down, are we?'

She thought at first he was sobbing until she heard him gasp for breath and giggle more openly.

'You're right—we're not!' he said firmly and then there was just the darkness and the sound of the eternal sea.

Margot had fancied she would sleep as her body made contact with the mattress, but she became more and more wide awake by the minute. Realising that there was no real need to sleep, as obviously there would be plenty of time for that, she allowed her mind to wander whither it would, and so she remembered all the events of that fateful day, from the confrontation with Guy to the moment the thugs had forced her to the floor of the minibus and held the ether pad over her face.

Guy had looked so—so ferocious, could one say?—as he had pulled her round to face him, and somehow in that ferocity was also the tenderness she knew him capable of. It was a gesture which demonstrated his feelings for her were still active, rather than the passive she had begun to suspect. He had minded her telling him he owed her nothing, and left her in no doubt with that one flash of angry communion that he believed *she* still owed *him* something, if only an explanation. Somehow this thought made her feel happier, not so cut off. Guy was up there somewhere, no doubt wondering where she was, and many others would be wondering, too.

She allowed her thoughts to drift on through all the party had done during the day, because somewhere, she was sure, there was a clue. It came as she remembered Van helping her to clear away after the alfresco lunch. He had said something about three men sitting among the rocks playing cards. 'Maybe they're murderers on the run,' he had said darkly, and she had thought how marvellous was the imagination of a child.

But maybe they were, if not murderers, criminals of another kind. The Italian newspapers reported at least one kidnapping every day. But George was not heir-apparent to some vast enterprise. The Whithams were comfortably off and lived well, but Mr Whitham was fond of saying he earned every penny he received, and that they were more often overdrawn at the bank than not. On the other hand his firm might be wealthy, and might offer to help.

Margot had no illusions but that she had been taken specifically to look after George. If they wanted him kept alive, for ransom, then he had to be cared for. Her abduction saved the kidnappers the job of looking after him themselves. Therefore they must have been acquainted with the fact that she was George's nurse. She was dressed in no way to advertise her profession, and yet their stores included a medical kit containing a syringe and morphia phials. She supposed in a real emergency she could put George safely to sleep or even kill him. Such tools in the hands of an amateur would have been akin to giving a child matches near a petrol dump. They knew what they were doing, obviously, and so they had observed and noted or been told.

This brought her back to Ricci, though grudgingly, and she tried to recall all she had seen him do during the day, from the moment he had complained of toothache on joining the bus to the time when he and the driver had lifted George up into the vehicle, and then he had said playfully to George, 'Now stop looking at those controls, boy! You are not driving the bus. Eh, Margot? You watch him. Yes? He got that look——' George had merely lifted his broad shoulders and Ricci had run back down the slope.

Then she saw the driver puffing on his cigarette, and immediately, to her amazement, a stranger stepped into the driver's seat. This turned to horror as she saw the man, Francesco, lying on the ground and those two awful, subhuman, stocking-masked faces gazing up at her. As a hand covered her mouth and she was dragged forward she had seen, for a moment, a face in the bushes, a familiar face belonging to Ricci.

Earlier Margot had doubted this vision, but now her subconscious projected until she saw him quite clearly. She could even take this vision out and study it, as one can freeze a television film to ascertain the truth of a vital portion of the action, and so she found herself in a subterranean cave, gazing at Ricci's face, surrounded by the yellow flowers of gorse, in her own memory, and noting that his expression was not so much one of horror as of urgency. It was as though he wished the action over so that he could step out and play his own part in it. But what part was that? she wondered. What was Ricci doing about securing their release if he had been a witness to the occurrence?

'He could have done something if he wanted to,' she decided morosely, trying not to think ill out of sheer habit.

There was no more, then, only the realisation and the necessity of looking after George and herself as best she could.

'So I'd better get some sleep,' she decided, and it was not too long before kindly nature obliged her.

'How long we been here?' George asked wearily.

'Two and a half days. I'm sorry, George, that I was wrong about us being rescued within hours. I was certain Ricci had seen those men and would have had the police on our track immediately. Shall we play another game? How about ordering our favourite meal in a good restaurant?'

'If you don't mind, Nurse, I'm not in the mood. Could I have one of those sleeping pills and pass a few more hours away?'

'Certainly, George. Here you are.' She sat by him until he fell asleep and then gave way to a feeling of utter desperation. She looked roofwards, where a round rock probably covered the hole through which they had been lowered, but even if she had had a ladder she doubted if her puny strength would have had any effect on it. Also they were growing weaker on the limited diet and it now bored them both. Margot took good care to give herself only half of what she fed to George, and now they had almost finished their second large bottle of mineral water. There were two more, and after them—what?

One night it must have rained, because Margot heard water trickling down one of the walls. Next morning she had found a pool had formed in a bowl-shaped depression, and so they both had a good wash. She then poured a little disinfectant from the first-aid bag into the water so that they could use it again, and again, until it evaporated. Sometimes she crawled down the tunnel and rattled the bars at the entrance, but failed to dislodge them. She would look out to sea. Once she came back and reported to George that a fishing boat had been passing. 'I took off my petticoat and waved it,' she said, 'but maybe nobody saw or thought it was just a bird fluttering.'

'I must keep calm and retain my confidence,' she now decided as firmly as she knew how. 'Somebody knows we're here. The people who put us here did it for money, no doubt, and we're no good to them dead.'

On the fifth day of their incarceration, Margot awoke unwillingly from a drugged sleep—she had resorted to taking an occasional sleeping pill from their store—trying not to immediately sink into the depths of despair. She saw that George was still asleep and felt afraid as she rose and her legs wobbled alarmingly. She was becoming very weak, though she tried to keep herself exercised by walking round and round the cave and climbing up and down on the various ledges, but exercise alone was not enough. She needed more food than she allowed herself.

For the first time she considered the possibility of dying, and that itself did not alarm her, the unknown being infinitely preferable to these present unbearable circumstances she now knew all too well. But if she died first then George would be frightened, and that really did worry her. She decided to talk frankly about these matters to George today, and ask him what she should do for him if there was a sudden deterioration in their physical condition. She scarcely had the energy nowadays to give him massage, and his legs were taking on an unhealthy blue tinge, which meant that the circulation was poor.

He awoke with a cry and she was beside him immediately, holding the neck of their last bottle of water to his lips. When that was finished there would be thirst, and often now, with the small drinks they took, they became extremely thirsty. It had not rained since that one night and so there had been no washes. Their clothes were filthy and smelly.

'Well, George, another day dawns,' she said with a forced smile. 'Today may be the day. Who knows?'

'Who knows, indeed, Nurse? I'm sore all over. Could you turn me over, please?'

'I've got a little alcohol left and I'll give you a rub.' She had lit the stub of a candle as not much daylight came into the cave. 'Yes, you are a bit sore there, but the skin's not broken. When I was in training, if we got a

patient with a bed-sore we were hauled before Matron.
That was the cardinal sin. Lie on your tummy for a bit,
while I get breakfast.'

'I don't want breakfast.' A maggot had crawled out of
the last of the cheese yesterday, and George had had
difficulty controlling his stomach thereafter. She couldn't
afford for him to vomit and lose precious fluids. 'Would
you think I was going soft if I said I'd turned to religion,
Nurse?'

'Not at all.'

'I'm saying my prayers again. Why is it we always wait
for something bad to happen before we do that seriously?'

'I think when human agencies are apparently helpless,
that we seek some higher Authority. We *have* to believe
in something,' Margot said steadily.

She didn't tell him about her nightmare, or could it
have been a delusion born of her weakness? In the night
she had shot upright, convinced that they were no longer
alone and that the presence she felt was malevolent. She
had been so frightened, convinced that a roll of thunder
had preceded her awakening. But there was something
more. There were noises and murmurings.

'Who's that?' she had called. 'Is anybody there? What
do you want?'

George had wakened and complained, 'What's with
you, Nurse? Let a guy sleep.'

The thunder had come again and dust suddenly
covered Margot's face, making her eyes water. She had
tried to clean herself up, now convinced that she had
suffered from an hallucination. Maybe a bat lived in the
cave and had been taking his nocturnal excursion.

'Do you have dreams, George?' she asked now.

'I guess so. They're getting a bit wild and woolly. Last night somebody was pushing my face into quicksand and I had to push back, but I was still going down. I woke up gasping, and had just got back into a peaceful sleep when you yelled out. Were you dreaming, too?'

'I must have been, but it seemed to me I was wide awake. I'm sorry I woke you. With these disturbed nights of ours we're waking up later and later. Would you believe it must be midday already? The sun's in the cave-mouth and I'm learning to tell the time by that. In an hour it's past its meridian and it leaves us. Have a biscuit, George. You must eat something.'

'Sorry, Nurse, no can do.'

'You make me worry about you,' she told him.

'Offer me a hot dog and I'd smack my lips, but I'm fed up with dry biscuits, chocolate and cheese.'

'Well, that's finished, and there're only two biscuits and four pieces of chocolate. Have another drink, then.'

'To please you,' he agreed. 'I say, Nurse, just in case we—you know? Well, we obviously can't go on for ever.'

'No. I was going to talk to you about that. I—I have stronger drugs. There's morphine. That can help in emergency.'

'Nurse, what *are* you saying? I was going to tell you that no matter what, I can take it. You're not to fret yourself about me. If I'm going to die, the least I can do is die like a gentleman. I think we should hold each other's hands, nights, from now on.'

'Oh, George!' Margot was weeping openly, and somehow it was such a relief. 'You've been magnificent, and

I want you to know it. In any normal relationship with you I could never have said a thing like that. I'm now going to force myself to eat a dry biscuit and a piece of chocolate so that I'll feel better able to look after you, and find the strength to move my mattress over to yours. As you say, from now on we'll hold hands every night.'

To overcome her emotion she did various domestic things. She had a damp hankie with which she wiped George's hands and face, and then she helped him off his stomach on to his side. They had both become used to the noise of the breakers against the cliff, but now she pricked her ears.

'I think a bird's caught in the bars, George. I'll go and look.'

She crawled down the tunnel entrance, which the sun was now leaving, and stared in astonishment. It must surely be another hallucination she was having, but she saw, quite distinctly, a newspaper package and a bottle of local red wine. Also—an absurdity—a fat piece of salami was stuck between the bars, smelling strongly of garlic. As the hallucination persisted she opened the newspaper package and there were two bread rolls filled with ham, four fat, misshapen tomatoes and two bananas. The package didn't dissolve in her hands, neither did the bottle. She tugged at the salami, but it wouldn't budge.

'George! George!' she yelled, taking her prizes with her. 'Tell me if I'm dreaming. What have I got here? Be very sure.'

He grinned. 'You've got a couple of bread rolls and some fruit, also a bottle of gut-rot with a screw top, and suddenly I feel very hungry.'

'So I'm not dreaming? And there's half of one of those strong, thick salamis stuck between the bars. Don't you see what this means, George? We're not forgotten. Somebody who knows these cliffs came down to feed us.' She couldn't help visualising Ricci. 'Don't eat too much at first, George. We'll wrap the rest up. You must eat a tomato, we both must be lacking Vitamin C. When I feel strong enough I'll have another tug at that sausage.'

The wine was new and very heady. After a couple of swigs each they were both lightheaded.

'Gosh, but I feel better for that,' Margot sighed. 'I think I'll have my afternoon nap. I'm quite drunk. How about you, George?'

But the boy was already nodding off, having drunk more than she, and she carefully removed the half sandwich from his unprotesting hand and wrapped up the remains of the feast. She felt most encouraged, as though there had been a sign from heaven. Later she would get the salami, but now she must sleep. She remembered to reach out for George's hand, as they had promised.

'Five days we've wasted now!' Guy ranted to himself. 'Five days when the kidnap squad could have been alerted and maybe come up with something. My good sense tells me that that idiot is turning himself loose with two hundred thousand used notes, and I ought to inform the authorities, but just supposing I did foul things up for him! God, I can't take much more of this. I can't do my job, I can't sleep. I look like the walking dead.'

He saw a bright blue and yellow bus pass the villa, and stared at the interested faces of what looked like a group of tourists from Scandinavia. The fact registered that Astria had only one tourist attraction, and in charge of that attraction was a young man he had found extremely elusive of late. Guy decided to join the party walking round the Terracini estate and suddenly had a sense of purpose, which was better than doing nothing.

Doctor Agostini's huge cross-bred dog, dutifully muzzled as the law required, leapt out of some bushes to join him. Guy greeted her fondly, realising he had neglected the poor creature lately. She must have escaped from the Agostini garden, and after he had talked to Signor Ricci Lamati he would take her back home again.

Guy and Teresa overtook the tourists as they were emerging from the little church and taking photographs. The dog was a great attraction, especially to the children of the party, and Ricci approached uncertainly.

'What do you want, Doctor?'

'I want to talk to you.'

'I got nothing to say. I too upset to talk about terrible tragedy. Also I got to work.'

'That's all right, I'm in no hurry. I'll wait.'

'No, don't wait! To see you upsets me and the dog shouldn't be in here.'

'Take your party round,' said Guy. 'Don't get so agitated, I only want to ask you a few simple questions.'

Ricci stalked off towards the castle, reciting facts and figures like an automaton suddenly. Guy remained in the background, determined not to be put off, but Teresa gambolled happily, as a big dog will, sniffing people and tussocks of grass and rocks with equal concentration.

Eventually the party began to drift back towards the main gates and their shining bus. They would now be running down to the village *trattoria* for refreshments.

Normally, Guy knew, Ricci did not accompany the party on this jaunt, but after seeing every member of the party aboard and receiving tips from many, the young Italian moved on to the bottom step of the bus as it started up and glared back at Guy, as though daring him to follow, as it moved off downhill.

Guy almost did follow; he felt like wringing Ricci's neck, and he was more than ever convinced that the fellow knew more than he was telling.

Now he looked at the disappearing bus and went back into the castle grounds, looking for Teresa, who was not in sight. Ricci had not even closed the gates in his haste to escape.

'Teresa!' Guy called. '*Avanti! Avanti!*'

There was a distant, deep, excited bark but no sight of the dog.

'I'll get her and proceed down to the village,' thought Guy. 'When I've delivered the dog I'll tell Giulio to hold the fort pending events. I'll find that boy and get the truth out of him somehow.'

Teresa was playing hard to get. She barked occasionally, and so Guy found himself on a narrow cliff ledge, the wind making his hair stand on end, as he watched the dog leaning over the edge of the cliff, maybe setting a gull, or something.

As Guy approached, to his horror, she slid over the edge with a barking sort of yelp. When he peered over he saw she was, mercifully, on a sort of small shelf about twelve feet below, and that a steep little track led down to this shelf. He hesitated to go down, however, as without a leash he would have difficulty in persuading Teresa to follow him back up to the top. She did not seem to be unduly troubled, for she had her nose up some rabbit hole or other, and was growling. Her rear end wagged excitedly. She reappeared to look up and back again, and then her front end again disappeared.

'She wants me to go down,' Guy decided, 'and what have I to lose, anyway?'

He slid over the edge of the cliff, not particularly worried about the rocks below as he had done plenty of cliff scrambling, and joined Teresa on the ledge, much to her delight. He was amazed upon lifting a tussock of grass to see an iron grille placed across a small cave mouth, securely bolted into the rocks on either side. Even this would not have surprised him as much as the sight of a great wedge of odorous salami shoved into the grille. Now that salami could only have got there by human agency, and it was this which was exciting Teresa so much. Food for the taking, and she with her muzzle on! Guy unbuckled the muzzle and Teresa tugged at the salami, her growling much more serious now that she had the use of her jaws.

Guy felt vaguely excited and hopeful. Either somebody outside had pushed the salami in for somebody inside, or the somebody inside had pushed the salami out—— No, that wasn't feasible. The salami, though smelling strongly of garlic, was fresh. It had been put there today to feed someone, and Guy felt sure it wasn't intended for the gulls.

'Margot!' he called through his hands, and above the din of the sea. 'Margot, for God's sake! If you're there, answer me!'

'Guy!' came thinly, from far away, and then he saw

her crawling towards him, laughing and crying at the same time. 'Oh, Guy! Guy!'

'That's all right, now, darling. Is George with you?'

'Yes—he's asleep. We're both O.K.'

'Well, listen, darling, I'm going to get help. I'll leave Teresa here. I'll be back within fifteen minutes. Don't go away!'

Emily Whitham scarcely recognised Doctor Massey. His shirt was torn and his hands bloody.

'I've found them!' he announced. 'They're O.K. They're in a cave under the castle.'

'Doctor, I'm going mad, I think. Did you say——?'

'I said I've found your son and *my* fiancée. I'm calling the police. Now, I have to know where your husband is. He did tell you, I hope? It's important. We don't want anything to happen to him now.'

Emily had collected herself from a drugged stupor as Guy spoke to the police in Leghorn, giving them the information they would require. Holding the receiver, Guy listened to the woman carefully and then continued speaking.

'And Mr Whitham is in a yellow taxi on the B.31 to Siena—yes, that's the old mountain road. The taxi-driver knows nothing, so far as Mrs Whitham knows, but her husband has a two hundred thousand dollar ransom in an old brown suitcase. He has been instructed to put it down by the Porgona T-junction and proceed twenty kilometres beyond. When he comes back he has been told the two young people will be waiting, but I don't see how that can be so. I'll leave things in your hands now, Captain, and go back to the cave. You'll find me over the cliff with a great white dog. If you could pick up Signor Ricci Lamati, in Astria, I'm sure he'll be able to help.'

So it was that Ricci, prodded not inconsiderably by several policemen and one angry detective, showed how it was possible to put a rope round a boulder among the ruins, and with considerable man effort pull it aside to reveal a hole in the roof of a cave. The Italian did not meet Margot's eyes as she was hauled clear in a harness the police had with them; she could not have seen him, in fact, for the light temporarily blinded her. A stretcher was waiting for George, but he was quite chirpy as he was brought out, and he did address Ricci.

'Hullo, old pal! I didn't know you were that hard up.'

'George, I swear, they made me,' Ricci said urgently. 'They threatened to kill me. I'm a good boy, you know that. Would I hurt my friend, do you believe? I brought you fresh food.'

Margot was in Guy's arms, and she never once questioned the fact. She felt as if she was floating on a cushion of air.

A young traffic policeman came on his motor-cycle across Ricci's sacred grass.

'They've found Whitham, in his taxi, still with the money,' said Guy relievedly, 'and caught the villains who took you.'

'Darling,' Margot asked from this strange other world she seemed to be occupying, 'would you mind most awfully if I fainted?' and without waiting for permission, she did so.

When Margot came to her senses again, she discovered that she was lying in a hospital bed. The bright sunshine was streaming in at the window and for a while she was content to bask in its warmth, barely able to believe that the terrible ordeal of the last few days was over and that she was safe at last.

At the sound of the door opening she turned her head and saw Guy standing there with a large bunch of freesias in his arms.

'Darling! You're awake at last!' He came towards her and sat down by her bedside. 'How do you feel?'

'I feel fine, all things considered,' Margot said, gazing happily up at him. Only a short while ago it had seemed that she would never see his face again, now they were together again and he was looking at her as if she was the only woman in the world. 'George—is he all right?'

'Yes, he's survived the experience remarkably well. That's probably due to your expert care. He's back with his family being fussed over and made the hero of the hour for his experiences.'

Margot laughed, then said soberly, 'It's a miracle that you found us, Guy. We were given fresh food, but I'm not sure how long either of us would have stood up to being kept in that cave for much longer.'

His arm was round her, reassuring her. 'It's all right, Margot, it's all over now. Treat it like a bad dream. The memory will fade.'

She buried her head in his shoulder, taking comfort in the fact that they were together again and that for once he was not rejecting her. But perhaps he just felt sorry for her. Perhaps, to him, the whole affair with her had been nothing but a casual experience—something to be forgotten, dismissed as quickly as he was telling her to forget the events of the past few days. She tried to pull away from him, but he only grasped her closer to him.

'Will you marry me, Margot? The Anglican bishop is here at the hospital and is willing to perform the ceremony. I've got the licence and all I need is your consent.'

'Marry you, Guy? But I don't understand? I thought you weren't able to marry me. I thought you didn't want to marry——'

'Not want to marry you?' Guy stopped her protests with a long kiss. 'Does that answer the question?'

Blushing slightly, she clung to him and answered shyly, 'Yes, but——'

'Margot, I wasn't able to explain everything to you before. I hoped that one day I might be free to ask you to marry me. I never gave up hope. But someone else had a claim upon me.'

'Your sister mentioned that there was a woman you once cared for who had come back into your life. I thought that perhaps you discovered that you still loved her,' Margot told him anxiously.

'Even Maxine couldn't be told the whole story.' He frowned at the memory and then explained to Margot. 'Yvonne Mountstewart and I were friends long before I met you. I was fond of her, but never loved her the way that she claimed to love me. I made it clear that I wouldn't have an affair with her—even if she was prepared to deceive her husband, I wasn't. She had no intention of leaving him, she loved the power and position that his name gave her. So we parted.'

He was silent for a moment and Margot prompted him gently, 'Then you met her again recently?'

'Yes. She was in a nearby clinic undergoing some

tests and she sent me a message asking me to visit her. I decided to go. She sounded desperate, as if I was her only friend in the world. I couldn't refuse to see her. Maxine thought the worst, of course, and told me not to be a fool. She thought that Yvonne was trying to recapture my interest by pretending to be ill.'

'I take it Maxine was wrong?' Margot asked softly.

'Yes. But she wasn't to know. It was the sort of trick that Yvonne had played before. I couldn't put her right about it. I couldn't even tell you, Margot, although I wanted to desperately. For the past few weeks I've been attending Yvonne as her doctor and therefore couldn't discuss her with anyone. I couldn't break a professional confidence by telling you that Yvonne was too ill to be capable of making a play for me—that all she wanted and needed were my professional services as a doctor.'

'Were you able to help her?'

He shrugged. 'She had lost weight. The tests confirmed what I suspected and—mercifully—she knew little about last week. She died peacefully, which was as much as I could do for her.'

Margot moved closer to him, offering him wordless sympathy.

He sighed. 'The grief I felt over losing Yvonne was nothing compared with the prospect of losing you, my darling. I thought I would go mad with worry about you. Just as it seemed that everything was going well between us and I was free to hand Maxine over to Paolo's care and able to marry you, everything went disastrously wrong again.'

'It's all over now and we're back together now,' she soothed. 'That's all that matters.'

'And you'll marry me immediately? The bishop is due in Rome and hasn't very long. I'm sorry to rush you.'

Margot laughed up at him as she swung her legs out of bed. 'It looks as if I'll have to agree, doesn't it! I only have my blue dress. Will that do?'

'Oh, my sweet! Of course it'll do. A sack would do.'

'I'll have to ask you to leave just one more time, Guy. While I get changed.'

'I'll be waiting just outside the door,' he told her. 'Mr Witham's giving you away and the rest of the family are in the chapel. They're flying home tonight.'

He put the freesias in her arms and bent to kiss her.

'I'll send Maxine in to help you dress. I'm sorry it's such a rush, but——'

Margot's eyes were wet as Guy's sister came in, smiling.

'Now I know what—what happy ever after means,' the young nurse said mistily. 'I always used to wonder.'

The freesias sent out a wave of approving fragrance, as though they knew the answer to that everlasting question, and the older woman nodded wisely, knowing full well that fairy tales do have a habit of coming true, if only you truly believe them.

Ex Libris